Paw, Claws, and Curses

PAW, CLAWS, AND CURSES

A Purr-fect Relic Cozy Mystery

DeAnna Drake

TULE
PUBLISHING

CHAPTER ONE

A Paw-ticular Problem

"I HAVE CLEOPATRA'S cat," a raspy, British guy croaked over the shop's phone.

A week ago, I would have hung up and dismissed the call as a prank, but since I'd arrived in Citrus Grove—a sleepy Southern California town that more closely resembled Mayberry than Malibu—I'd learned to expect the unexpected. That was especially true here in my grandfather's shop, where he technically sold antiques, just not the typical variety. There were no vintage gramophones or old silver tea sets. No tin lunch boxes with Scooby-Doo and the gang.

His antiques and what he called *faux relics*—he also allowed the term *replicas* but definitely not *fakes*, I'd learned that the hard way—leaned more toward the Hollywood prop shop variety. Imagine the kind of things someone would see on the sets of those adventure movies featuring ancient artifacts and chiseled, whip-cracking hotties.

Since I was here at least partly because the shop's former manager had swiped some family heirlooms my grandfather had inherited from his globe-trotting granddad, which included an old feline figurine from Egypt, the caller had my complete attention.

"Hold on a sec. I'll get the owner." I set down the phone's receiver and poked my head out of the back office to look for Stirling, but he was already gone.

"Sorry about that," I said when I picked up the phone again. "He seems to have stepped out, but I can help you."

"Who are you?" the caller barked.

"I'm Rebecca. I'm—"

"No. I need to speak with Stirling." The caller coughed and continued in a voice even hoarser than before. "When will your grandfather be back?"

"How did—" I stopped.

I might be new to Cuthbert Exotic Antiques, but I'd spent the better part of my twenty-six years behind a cash register, and I knew it wasn't good business to question customers, even if they were rude and claimed to have stolen property. Still, I'd only learned Stirling was my grandfather two weeks ago, so how could the caller possibly know?

"What I mean is," I continued, assuming the man must know Stirling and had heard about our recent reunion, "we're happy to hear the item is safe. If you'll give me your name and number, I'll have my grandfather return your call as soon as possible."

Another cough filled the line. When it subsided, the caller said, "I need him here. Now."

That was not a British accent. Maybe Australian? What I knew for sure was the frustration in the man's voice was growing by the second.

Talk about bad timing. It had taken me all day to persuade my grandfather to go home and rest. He'd said he was just a little tired after a bad night's sleep, but people who were only a little tired didn't fall asleep while making tea or while watching an online auction for ancient Egyptian faience beads.

Okay, maybe the auction was a snoozer, but by three, the poor guy didn't even have the energy to push his wire-rimmed bifocals back into place. For an hour, they sat teetering on the end of his nose.

When I caught him snoring in front of the computer, I nudged him awake and assured him I'd been helping my parents run their bookstore since I was old enough to see over the counter. I promised I'd been paying attention when he and I closed the shop together the past few nights and that I was more than capable of handling it alone.

He reluctantly agreed to head home, probably because we hadn't had a single customer all day, anyway.

But now, not fifteen minutes after his exit, this happened.

"May I put you on hold?" I asked the anxious caller. "I'll see if I can track him down."

I dialed the landline in Stirling's apartment, the only option since he didn't own a cell phone. He lived a few doors away, in an apartment above a barbershop, so I expected him to pick up.

He didn't. After eight rings, I hung up and bit my thumbnail. What would Stirling want me to do? We rarely discussed the theft or the ex-manager behind it. My grandfather had only mentioned it in passing when he'd called that first time after the funeral because he wanted me to know why he couldn't come to Montana to meet me.

He couldn't leave town, he'd said, because he was hoping the police would track down the thief and retrieve his stolen property.

Even in that short conversation, I'd felt the magnitude of his loss. When he said the stolen items were part of a personal collection that held mostly sentimental value, it reminded me of my father. He'd kept a box under his bed that was filled with tattered volumes of ancient histories and myths that would never be considered valuable in the traditional sense, yet they meant the world to him.

I sensed the same devotion in Stirling, and it made me wonder what other qualities they shared and what had kept them apart all these years. I suppose that was one reason I said yes when Stirling asked if I'd be interested in visiting him.

The fact that I needed a distraction from my own problems sealed the deal. Helping my newfound grandfather navigate this difficult time in his life meant I wouldn't have to navigate my own, at least for a while.

I switched the line back to the caller. "I couldn't reach him, but the shop closes in an hour. Can I take a message? I'll be sure he gets it."

"Yes! I must see him as soon as possible."

I thought the guy was going to jump through the receiver.

After another coughing fit, he added, "The name is Gunther Vernon. He knows me. Tell him to come as soon as he can."

"Does he have your address?"

He gave it to me, and I scribbled it on a yellow sticky note.

"It's urgent. Understand?"

Normally, I'd push back on a pushy customer, but this guy was trying to return something that belonged to Stirling. So, I let it slide and assured him I was happy to help.

It was the truth. Getting that heirloom back would make Stirling's day, and that made me want to drop everything and run to his apartment to deliver the good news. But I still had a shop to watch, so I had to be patient.

Unfortunately, patience wasn't my strong suit.

To distract myself from the ticking clock, I filled the shop's electric kettle with water and browsed through the drawer full of colorful boxes and bags of tea. Coffee was my preferred source of caffeine, but my grandfather was a tea drinker, so for the past few days I'd been trying to make do. I'd tried a few different varieties, and so far, the Scottish breakfast tea was my favorite. It was nearly as robust as coffee, offered a noticeable jolt of caffeine, and was so smooth it didn't need sugar.

You only live once, though, so I still added a couple tea-spoons of the sweet stuff after dropping the tea bag into a cup and dousing it with the almost-boiling water from the kettle.

Despite the diversion, I couldn't stop thinking about the phone call and Stirling. So, I did what I always do when I'm nervous or stressed or both. I cleaned. I found a dust cloth in the storage room—which was really more of a closet—and got to work.

My grandfather kept a tidy shop. All the tiny statues of Egyptian gods were arranged in neat rows in the cabinets, an assortment of turquoise and carnelian collar necklaces and bracelets were carefully displayed in a glass case, and the brass lanterns hung attractively from the ceiling. Everything had its place.

But dust was everywhere. In some spots, it was hardly noticeable, like the counter near the cash register. Other places had a layer so thick you could see a trail when you dragged a fingertip through it. Those were the areas I went after, with occasional pauses for a sip of tea.

The stuff wasn't half bad once I got used to it.

I cleaned and nursed my tea until something occurred to me. A concern, actually, tangled in a question. Why disturb my exhausted grandfather and send him off to retrieve something I could easily get myself?

Not only that, but Gunther Vernon was also obviously sick, so exposing Stirling to that couldn't be a good idea. He seemed to be an exceptionally healthy septuagenarian, but why take the chance of getting him infected with whatever that man had? My grandfather would need a ride to the man's place anyway since Stirling didn't own a car.

I should just go myself. It made more sense, and it would be a nice surprise for him. Getting back one of his stolen items was the least I could do to thank him for all the warm hospitality he'd shown me since I'd arrived.

I stared at the address on the yellow sticky note. *Five forty-two South Partridge Lane.* I pulled out my phone and typed in the address. A red pin on a map marked a spot several blocks away.

Close, but not within walking distance. Stirling would definitely need a ride.

Closing time was still a half-hour away, but what were the chances anyone would come in now when the shop had been deserted all day? None, I told myself as I rinsed my cup in the washroom sink, flipped the open sign to closed, and locked the doors.

Once I reached my faded blue Subaru hatchback, parked on the street a half a block away, there was no looking back. If Stirling returned to the shop and found me gone, he'd forgive me when he saw his Cleopatra's cat. That was what mattered.

At least I hoped it was.

CHAPTER TWO

The Open Door

S ITTING BEHIND THE wheel, I pulled up the map on my phone again. I had a pretty good idea where I was going, but I didn't want to take any chances. I'd already gotten lost a few times because Orange County streets had a strange way of twisting and turning or stopping altogether in one place and starting again in another. I could do without those kinds of surprises.

It wasn't like back home. When a person grew up in a mountain town like Elk Pass, Montana, there were no surprises.

Not with the streets, anyway.

But this wasn't the time to dwell on that. Instead, I focused on the directions.

It would have been easier if I hadn't had to sit at the red light near Malone's Diner, where an A-frame sign on the sidewalk trumpeted spaghetti night, featuring Mama Malone's homemade sauce. Even with the windows rolled up, the savory smells coming out of that place were making my mouth water.

Since Stirling probably wouldn't be going out for his usual evening meal, which tended to be Malone's anyway, I made a mental note to stop in on the way back to grab a couple spaghetti orders to take back to the apartment. The freezer meal I'd microwaved for lunch was a distant memory, so a hearty mound of pasta with a side of meatballs sounded like absolute heaven.

I was still lost in that marinara-fueled fantasy when my phone's screen announced I'd reached my destination.

It was a residential neighborhood that looked like many I'd seen on this side of town, with rows of cozy Craftsman-style bungalows, mature eucalyptus trees, and, of course, palm trees. This was Southern California, after all.

But when I found Gunther Vernon's street number, I had to double-check my directions because there had to be a mistake. Nope, this was the right place.

A sinking feeling crept over me.

From the street, the only thing visible over the thick, towering hedge was the top of a giant magnolia tree and the peaked roof of the dark, two-story Victorian house behind it.

Even in the daylight, the place gave off serious horror-movie vibes.

Night came earlier here than it did back home, but there was at least another hour before darkness fell, and I was thankful for it. Instead of focusing on the creepy factor, I rehearsed what I would say when the guy opened the door and found me instead of my grandfather. I'd decided to start by telling him Stirling wasn't feeling well and quickly add that I knew he was in a hurry and didn't want to make him wait.

I'd been sure that would win him over, but now I had my doubts.

By the time I parked and let myself through the black wrought-iron gate, I was rethinking my whole plan. All I really wanted to do was crawl back into my car and forget the whole thing.

I didn't feel any better when I got a look at what that ten-foot-tall hedge was hiding. To call it a house was an understatement. It was more like one of those dark and moody monstrosities that loomed over the desolate English moors in gothic novels.

Although teenage me—the one who'd been consumed by the Bronte sisters' novels—was secretly hoping to find Heathcliff striding about on the other side, the older and wiser me knew I was far more likely to find someone, or something, Edgar Allan Poe might have dreamed up.

There was still time to turn around. I glanced back at the sliver of street I could see beyond the gate. I could be out of here and placing that spaghetti order in five minutes flat.

But then I thought of Stirling and that smile I wanted to see on his face when I handed him his stolen treasure.

I didn't need to be a hero like one of those adventure movie heartthrobs I daydreamed about as I cleaned Stirling's shop or even the inimitable Adelaide Morris, the Victorian spinster-turned-archaeologist-turned-amateur sleuth featured in my favorite mystery novels, which was probably more my speed. But I needed something good to happen for a change. After the accident and the funeral and the stupid canceled wedding, after everything that'd gone wrong, wasn't it about time for something to go right?

A gentle breeze rustled the magnolia tree's leaves over my head. Was it a sign to keep going?

My gut told me it was.

So, I pushed my tangled dark curls off my shoulders, tugged my pale-blue Oxford shirt straight, and marched up the porch steps to the veranda that wrapped halfway around the house. When I raised my knuckles to the door, I saw it was already ajar. I knocked anyway.

No one answered, so I tried again.

Still nothing.

"Hello? Mr. Vernon, are you there?" This time I pounded with the side of my fist.

More silence, but my pounding had pushed the door farther open, so I peeked inside. A checkerboard of black and white marble tiles led to a mahogany staircase on one side of the hall. An archway on the other side revealed the front room. At the very back, I could just make out French doors overlooking a garden.

Still, the only sounds came from the street.

"Hello?" I stepped over the threshold to see inside. Who

lived like this? The place was like a museum, with a ruby velvet settee, matching tufted chairs, and Tiffany lamps on the side tables.

While the furnishings would have been right at home in a Dickens novel, the decor was something else entirely.

Covering every wall and tabletop were the strangest items. Fossilized bones and figurines, ancient vases and bowls, even some framed fragments of ancient papyrus. An odd and eclectic collection, even by Cuthbert Exotic Antiques' standards.

Adelaide Morris would have a field day. I, on the other hand, would prefer to read about places like this than actually pay them a visit.

Yet, if there was an Egyptian cat statue to be found, this seemed a likely place. That was what I told myself as I ventured inside. Gunther Vernon had to be around somewhere, maybe upstairs or out back. I didn't like barging into a stranger's home, but the sooner I retrieved this Cleopatra's cat, the sooner I could leave.

"Is anyone here?"

Still not a peep. If the man was upstairs, I'd probably hear him moving around, and I didn't, so I decided to check the garden.

As I moved down the hallway alongside the staircase, I marveled at a collection of primitive masks displayed on the wall. When I reached an open door to a side room, light spilled out of it. I glanced in and saw it was a library or maybe a home office, it was difficult to say for sure because of the state of the place.

Books and vases and bowls had been pulled off the bookshelves that lined the walls and left in a heap on the floor. Animal skulls and carved figurines were strewn across the space as well. Crates and boxes had been upended, with their contents and packing material tossed about in complete disarray.

Someone had thoroughly ransacked the room.

As I wondered who could have done such a thing, I realized I wasn't alone. The man was dressed in a beige linen suit with tan leather loafers, and I would have instantly begged his forgiveness for trespassing if he hadn't been lying motionless on the floor.

I didn't want to jump to conclusions, but if that dark red substance pooling near his head was what I thought it was, I was pretty sure the poor man was dead.

CHAPTER THREE

Detective Scowls-a-Lot

"**Y**OU WERE HERE looking for a cat?"

It was the second time Detective Nick Devon of the Citrus Grove Police Department had asked me that question. This time, he stopped scribbling in his notepad and aimed his steel-gray eyes at me like they were cannons ready to fire.

"A statue of a cat." I stared at the front bay window beside us to avoid that glare. "It's from Egypt." As if that made a difference. "But yes, like I told the other officer. Gunther Vernon called me about an hour ago and told me he had it. He wanted my grandfather to come by to pick it up, but he wasn't available, so I came. You will let me look for it when we're done here, right?"

Discovering the body had rattled me so much I'd completely forgotten why I was here until the first pair of officers arrived. I'd waited for them on the porch, and before I knew it, there were police and other uniformed people swarming all over the place. It was impossible to get back into the study to search for my grandfather's stolen property.

The detective's scowl gave me little hope we would be wrapping up anytime soon.

"You came to a suspected thief's house by yourself?" His tone reeked of disapproval, and his left eyebrow arched skyward in disgust.

Or maybe disbelief. Either way, it made me want to melt into the floor and disappear. It hadn't even occurred to me that Gunther Vernon might be involved in the theft or that I could have been in danger.

"Why would he want to return it if he was the one who stole it? Besides, my grandfather already knows who the thief is. It was his shop manager. Or former manager. The guy's name is Martin Fincher, and your department is already looking for him. I don't know how Gunther ended up with the statue, but I figured he was trying to be a good Samaritan."

The detective ran his finger over his scruffy beard, which was a shade lighter than his short chestnut hair. "Good Samaritan. Right. Got it."

I knew sarcasm when I heard it. "Look, maybe you think that's naïve, but where I come from, we don't assume strangers are criminals."

Was there a note of condescension in my voice? You bet there was. I didn't appreciate being talked to like I was a child. By the look of him, he wasn't much older than I was. Maybe thirty, tops.

My tone wasn't having the desired effect, though. Detective Scowls-a-Lot sucked in his cheeks and tried to hide his irritation with another rub across his chin. "And where are you from, exactly?"

My fingers curled into frustrated fists at my side. "Elk Pass, Montana."

"Hm." He made a note.

Maybe I wasn't getting through to him. I tried again. "The thing was stolen from my grandfather's antique shop a few weeks ago. I'm trying to get it back. He's been helping me through a difficult time, and I thought it would be a nice way to thank him, you know, under the circumstances."

The detective's glance popped up again. "What circumstances are those, Mrs. Cuthbert?"

The title made me cringe. "It's Miss Cuthbert. I'm not married."

At least I'd dodged that bullet.

"Right, Miss Cuthbert, and the circumstances?"

I didn't even know where to start. I suppose I could tell him about losing both of my parents in a freak car accident. Or finding out my fiancé was a no-good, cheating jerk. Or that my best friend since kindergarten was no better. I doubted the good detective wanted to hear about any of that, so I told him the only part that seemed relevant. "Stirling Cuthbert has been letting me stay with him while I'm in town. Since his shop is shorthanded, you know, because his ex-manager is a criminal, I've been helping out."

The detective straightened, and oh boy, was he tall. I was five-foot-five in my sneakers, but my nose barely reached his shoulders. They were surprisingly broad shoulders, too, which made his navy-blue polo shirt with the police department logo on the chest a snug fit. Probably a weightlifter, like Mason. Probably a self-obsessed snake who said he was going to the gym when he was really sneaking around with...

"Wait. Is your grandfather Stirling Cuthbert of Cuthbert Exotic Antiques downtown?"

The question pulled me from my inner rant. "Yeah, that's him." There was no point dwelling on the past, I reminded myself. It was a thousand miles away, and it couldn't hurt me now anyway. Not anymore.

"I suppose that explains the Egyptian cat, then." The detective's lips quirked into a smile.

He was sort of cute when he smiled like that, despite the bulging muscles.

"Something wrong, Miss Cuthbert?" He lifted that quizzical eyebrow again.

Heat crept over my cheeks. "No, Detective. I was, uh..." What was the question? "The cat. Right. So, you're familiar with my grandfather's shop."

"Sure. It's near the traffic circle. Been there forever, hasn't it?"

"I think so."

A bronze plaque near the shop's front door said it had been established by Jerome Percival Cuthbert in 1922. I assumed the Cuthbert family—a family I knew nothing about—had run the shop ever since, and from the looks of it, probably changed very little.

But then, none of the buildings in Citrus Grove's historic district seemed to have changed much in at least fifty years. I imagined it was that old-fashioned charm that attracted the crowds to the antique shops that filled the neighborhood, along with the vintage clothing shops, the memorabilia store next door, and the retro-inspired restaurants like Malone's Diner.

At first, I didn't know what to make of the place. When I left my Rocky Mountain home for Orange County, California, I was envisioning sandy beaches and breaking waves.

But instead of something like Surf City USA, I found Main Street USA. It wasn't what I'd expected, but the place was growing on me.

The detective gave me another curious look. "You only think so? You don't know?"

"No, sorry. I didn't even know Stirling until recently. He found me a couple weeks ago."

He didn't say anything, but the line between his eyebrows deepened.

A wave of doubt swept through me. Did he think I was lying? Did he think I had something to do with this man's death? From his point of view, I had to admit it didn't look good. I mean, who strolled into a stranger's house without permission? Why couldn't Gunther Vernon have been clutching his chest from a heart attack or something? Even a slippery floor would have been better.

Instead, there was that pool of blood and no reasonable explanation for it.

The second I'd seen it, my gut told me the man was dead, but I still tried to rouse him, which meant evidence of my *crime-scene tampering*—an officer's words, not mine—were all over the place. My bloody sneaker prints on the floor, strands of my long, dark hair, and who knew what else.

All I could say in my defense was, I wasn't thinking about the crime scene when I found him. I was trying to wake him up. It sounded silly now, but I had really hoped he was only unconscious.

But he wasn't. Gunther Vernon was dead.

Still, what did the detective expect? I'd never seen a dead body before. I hadn't even seen my parents. After the car accident, the coroner told me the fire had consumed everything. She'd tried to soften the news by saying it probably hadn't been the flames that killed them, but the impact of the car skidding across the icy road and tumbling off the cliff.

My jaw tensed as I pushed away the pain of that memory. *It's all a thousand miles away. It can't touch me. Not here.* I focused on the detective, who was scribbling in his notepad again.

His pen paused. "I guess I'm still wondering why you

went inside if Mr. Vernon was already dead when you arrived, as you say."

There was that sinking feeling again.

"When I saw the open door, I poked my head in and thought he might be in the backyard. I walked through to look. As I passed that room, I saw him. I thought he'd fallen, and I wanted to help."

He scowled again.

"Isn't that what normal people do? Try to help someone if they're hurt or in trouble, even if it's a complete stranger?" I cringed at how defensive I sounded and crossed my arms over my chest. "I'm sorry. It's been a long day. Are we almost done?"

One of the first officers to respond, a surfer type with sun-bleached hair, walked up and leaned into the detective's ear. "The coroner needs to speak with you."

"I'll be there in a minute." Detective Scowls-a-Lot closed his notepad and tucked his pen through the metal spiral.

The officer nodded and went back to the kitchen.

As he did, a white-haired woman in a simple gray dress and black, sensible shoes stormed through the front door and stared in horror at the scene inside. "What is going on here? Where is Mr. Vernon?"

That accent, what was it? It reminded me of Gunther Vernon's, but I still couldn't place it. German, maybe? Or Nordic?

Her pale features gave little clue as she marched down

the hall, demanding answers and complaining about the dirt being tracked through the house. She stopped in front of the detective and glared up at him with her fists on her hips. "What is the meaning of this?"

She was a small slip of a thing, but somehow her presence filled the room. Still, if her intention was to intimidate him, it wasn't working. He glared right back at her.

"Who are you," he demanded, "and what is your relationship to Mr. Vernon?"

"Eva Henriksen. I manage this house." She gave me a curious glance, as if wondering if I mattered. She must have decided I didn't because she turned back to the detective. "Has there been a break-in? I told Mr. Vernon not to keep his inventory in the house. These things are too valuable. I told him a hundred times. It was that horrible cat thing, wasn't it? I knew it was trouble the instant I laid eyes on it. I have a sense about these things, you know. I always have."

Detective Devon gritted his teeth. "If you would kindly step into the dining room, an officer will assist you." He gestured down the hall and motioned to the officer who had delivered the coroner's message. "Please take the housekeeper's information."

"Excuse me! I am a domestic manager, not a housekeeper." The woman huffed and gave the detective a long, frosty look.

"Of course, ma'am," he said. "My apologies." I caught him rolling his eyes as she followed the officer, then he turned back to me. "Could you wait here a moment?"

The sky was slipping into darkness, and I'd already told him everything I had to say. "Can't I go? It's getting late."

He looked at me like I'd asked for a round-trip ticket to Paris. "You can't leave. I need you to walk me through what happened one more time."

Was he serious?

"We've already been over that. Twice. Even they heard me." I motioned to a pair of uniformed officers guarding the door, who had glanced up when I raised my voice, and the crime lab technician, who had entered with what looked like a toolbox and a duffel bag. "Everyone here knows what happened."

The detective smirked and shook his head. "I'd still like to hear it again."

So, it was like that, huh? I narrowed my eyes on him. "Fine. I was here to get my grandfather's stolen statue. The door was open, I came in, I saw a dead body, and I called you guys. That's it. Now can I go?"

Detective Devon was only half listening to me because the interview taking place in the back was getting loud. Very loud.

"Of course, I don't know what happened to Mr. Vernon," Eva Henriksen bellowed. "You saw me walk in. How could I know anything? What about that woman? Who is she?"

I peeked around Detective Devon and saw that diminutive lady advancing on the officer. Every time he stepped back, she stepped forward and thrust her pointed finger at his tanned face. She might be small, but she was ferocious. I wondered if the officer needed help.

Detective Devon must have wondered the same thing when he glanced back. "Fine," he said to me. "I'll have Officer Meadows finish your paperwork." He turned back to the officer and yelled, "Meadows, may I see you, please?"

The officer backed away from the older woman and hurried to the detective. "Yes, sir?"

"Please get Mrs. Cuthbert's information."

"Ms." I corrected. "Or Miss. But definitely not Mrs."

Detective Devon's lips pulled into a straight, irritated line. "Yes. Of course, Miz Cuthbert."

The mockery was obvious, but I didn't care.

"Sure, detective." The officer patted his shirt pocket, then his pants pockets.

Detective Devon sighed. "Here." He handed the man his pen, then turned to me. "Come down to the station in the morning. We'll finish the interview then."

"I can't."

"Excuse me?" He shot me a scathing look.

"I have to be at the shop." Maybe that wasn't exactly true, but I wasn't going to be at this man's beck and call, either. I didn't do anything wrong, and a girl had limits. I'd reached mine.

That eyebrow shot skyward again. "The shop opens at

ten, if I recall correctly. I'll be at my desk by seven-thirty. If you come in before eight, you'll be done in plenty of time. Otherwise, I can arrest you. Let me know which you prefer."

I knew a scare tactic when I heard one, but I was tired of arguing. I was tired, period. "Fine. I'll meet you at eight, as long as you promise I'll be out by nine-thirty."

"We'll call it a goal," he groused.

Before I could argue, Eva Henriksen stormed by, her chin jutted up and her arms straight as razors at her side.

"Excuse me," Detective Devon called out and lurched after her. "You can't leave."

She didn't stop. She didn't even slow down until she reached the door. Detective Devon followed her.

I considered navigating around them and slipping out before he changed his mind about letting me go, but as long as he was distracted, there was something I needed to do first.

CHAPTER FOUR

Broken Pieces

WHILE DETECTIVE DEVON had Eva Henriksen cornered, he wasn't watching me. As far as I could tell, no one was, so I strolled down the hall. When I neared the ransacked room, I lingered at the collection of African masks and waited while two men covered Gunther Vernon's dead body with a black plastic sheet. Once they had strapped him to a stretcher and wheeled him through the door, I poked my head inside.

The room was empty.

Carefully, I looked around. Everyone seemed preoccupied, so I ducked into the study to search for anything resembling an Egyptian cat statue.

It had to be somewhere in this mess. I tried the desk first. That was where the body had been, and I figured Gunther Vernon would have had it close since he was expecting my grandfather. But there was no sign of anything feline, just a half-eaten cheeseburger and some ketchup and fries piled on a Malone's takeout bag. Considering it was his last meal, the guy could have done worse, though I personally would have preferred the French dip myself, which was almost as good as my mom's.

As I continued to search, I felt a little like Adelaide Morris searching through the rubble of some lost Egyptian temple for clues that would help her catch whichever tomb-raiding master criminal she was chasing.

This wasn't a temple, but the treasures were real enough. Unlike Cuthbert Exotic Antiques, there didn't seem to be any faux relics here. Only artifacts that looked like they belonged in a natural history museum. As I sifted through, searching for anything that looked like a cat, I could hear Detective Devon questioning the older woman.

"Can you think of anyone who would want to hurt your employer?"

"No one comes to mind, but I always told him to be careful. These things belong in a gallery, where they can be protected. But did he listen? Of course not. This week was different, though. He usually keeps his office door open, but for the past few days, it's been locked. He's been hiding in there like a hermit. Always on the phone or the computer. Very strange."

"Excuse me, detective. The coroner needs you to release the body, so we can get it to the morgue." It was a man's voice at the door. "Could we get a signature?"

There was a pause then something that sounded like the stretcher being wheeled onto the porch.

And then a sob. No, not a sob. This was a full-blown blubber fest.

I peeked out of the room and spotted the detective standing awkwardly near the older woman. She held her face in her hands.

"I can't believe this happened," she wailed. "He was not a good man, not really, but he didn't deserve this."

"No one deserves this, ma'am." He touched her shoulder awkwardly. "I know it's a difficult time, but I do have a few more questions."

Did that man ever run out of questions?

The woman sniffled and wiped tears from her eyes. "Yes, fine. Whatever you need."

I went back to my search but kept an ear on their conversation.

"What line of work was Mr. Vernon in?" the detective asked.

"Art imports, mostly. Ancient art and artifacts. Look around. It's all here."

She was right about that. The house contained so many odd trinkets and treasures, it put my grandfather's shop to shame.

"Do you know what prompted the sudden secrecy?" the detective pressed. "Was he working on something in particular?"

"There was a cat figurine. An old, ugly, horrible-looking thing. Egyptian, I believe. That's when the trouble started.

I'll show you."

I stiffened. Were they coming in here? Was the detective about to catch me mid-snoop? I rushed into the dark shadow behind the door.

"It was right here." The woman marched in, with the detective close behind, and went straight to a display cabinet covered in upended vases and figurines. I recognized some of them as ancient Egyptian and Mayan in origin, but others I didn't recognize at all.

When I peeked from the shadows, the woman was tapping an empty space on a shelf. "It was here. He was obsessed with it. The professor didn't like it, though. I heard them arguing over it yesterday. Things became quite heated, as I recall."

"Do you recall this professor's name?"

"Of course. It's Dr. Abraham Omar. They used to work together in the archeology department at the university years ago, and Mr. Vernon hires him as a consultant now and then, usually to track down information about the older, more obscure pieces."

"Was Professor Omar here often?"

"No, but he was here yesterday. He arrived as I was finishing up for the day. I don't usually pay attention to their conversations, but I remember I was surprised that he seemed so impressed with that horrid cat."

"Why would you say he was impressed?"

"He told Mr. Vernon not to sell it, not for any price,

which I thought was odd, considering it looked worthless to me. Still, Mr. Vernon was having none of it. He called the professor a stupid, superstitious man. They went back and forth quite vigorously. You see, Mr. Vernon already had a buyer set up and was quite pleased about the price. He'd been bragging about it for days."

Obviously, the woman was mistaken. Mr. Vernon wasn't going to sell it, he intended to return it. Was she lying, or did she just get it wrong? Maybe the man had changed his mind.

The detective had other concerns. "So, it was valuable, this cat figurine?"

"I suppose so, but I can't imagine why. I'll show you. It must be here somewhere." She picked up a bronze Hindu god that had tipped over on the display case and set him upright before doing the same with a skull made of deep-blue glass. "Did your people really have to make such a mess of things?"

"I would apologize, but we didn't do this. This is how we found it."

She glanced around and shook her head. "Mr. Vernon would never do this. He had his faults, but he was not messy."

"We think he might have struggled with his attacker. But the cat figurine that you mentioned, are you sure it was here?"

"Yes. Why? Have you seen it? He kept it here." She

tapped the shelf again.

"Would you describe it?" he asked.

"Brown. Dusty. About this big." She held her hands about a foot's length apart. "There were black markings for the eyes and mouth and little ears, but it was so worn and chipped it was difficult to say for sure."

"Like that?" The detective pointed to the floor beside the desk.

From my hiding place, I followed his finger but couldn't see what he meant.

The woman could, though. She moved closer and bent down. "Oh, goodness. It must have fallen. What a shame."

My heart broke. So much for reuniting my grandfather with his lost treasure.

"Perhaps the pieces can be reassembled," she said and reached out to gather them.

"Please don't touch anything." Detective Devon hurried to the door and called out, "We've found something. Could I get a fingerprint kit?"

Instantly, a man in a blue cap and windbreaker entered with a toolbox.

"Over here." The detective pointed to the statue's remains.

While he and Eva Henriksen watched the technician work, I quietly tiptoed out of my hiding place and hurried out of the house.

Outside, I kept my eyes down and focused on my escape,

ignoring the stretcher rolling into the coroner's van and all the crime-scene tape. I ignored everything until I settled behind my car's steering wheel, put the key into the ignition, and held it there.

As much as I wanted to get away from this dreary place, with its gruesome dead body and that irritating detective, I was dreading having to tell my grandfather the sad fate of his prized possession even more.

If only I had arrived earlier. Maybe Gunther Vernon would still be alive, and maybe Cleopatra's cat would still be in one piece.

A little voice inside whispered, *or maybe the killer would have attacked you, too.*

A cold shiver ran down my spine.

Puttering around my grandfather's strange antiques and faux relics sometimes made me feel like I'd stepped into an adventure movie or one of Adelaide Morris's mysteries, but I knew I was no hero. Not even close.

All it took was one dead body and one broken cat statue to make that point abundantly clear.

What I really wanted to do was get back to Stirling's place and crawl into that cozy guest bed he was letting me use.

I turned the ignition key and let the rumbling engine calm my frayed nerves.

Slowly, I guided the car down the dark street and back toward the shop. When I turned onto the main street and saw the red neon sign of Malone's in the distance, I wondered if an extra-large order of spaghetti would help to soften the blow. For both of us.

A strange sound interrupted my thoughts. A low, whining kind of sound from the engine. Or was it the brakes?

Who was I kidding? I knew next to nothing about cars. Dad had always handled my car troubles. Or Mason.

It couldn't be too bad, though. There were no warning lights screaming at me from the dashboard, and I'd had the oil changed last … honestly, I couldn't remember the last time I'd had it changed. That was probably the problem.

I pulled to the side of the road and listened more carefully. The sound didn't repeat.

Had I imagined it?

I turned the engine off and listened again.

Nothing.

Then there was something. A soft, guttural sort of whimper, but it wasn't coming from the engine. It was behind me.

And whatever it was, it sounded alive.

CHAPTER FIVE

Surprise Visitor

M Y FINGERS TIGHTENED on the steering wheel as I considered my options. Fish my phone from my purse and dial 911? Use the purse to beat the intruder to a pulp? Jump out of the car and scream?

Before I could do anything, another throaty, groaning sound triggered the flight in my fight-or-flight response. I grabbed the door handle and exited the car as quickly as possible.

Once I was clear, I searched the sidewalk for a stick, a stone, anything I could use as a weapon.

Nothing.

I regretted not pulling my keys from the ignition. I'd read in an old self-defense manual about holding them between your fingers like spikes. Not as good as a bat or pepper spray, but better than nothing, which was what I had.

Adrenaline coursed through me as I crouched, ready to run, but I couldn't actually see anyone in my back seat. They had to be lying on the floorboard. From a few paces away, I called, "Who's in there?"

I didn't expect an answer, but I hoped to at least draw the intruder out.

Nothing stirred. I crept closer to peer through the window and found the back seat empty. It didn't make sense.

Had I imagined the sound?

To be safe, I slid the seat forward to check underneath.

That was when I saw the scraggly bundle of matted gray fur curled up in a ball. A tiny ear flicked and a heavy-lidded pair of blue eyes blinked up at me.

It was a kitten. A small, feral kitten by the look of it.

My fear—and my heart—melted.

"You poor, little thing." I bent down to stroke the fur on its head. "How did you get in here?"

Had it crawled in when I wasn't looking? I wasn't sure how it could have managed it, but I had been distracted. The creature was probably terrified. Except it didn't look terrified. It looked exhausted and half asleep.

I moved aside, making a clear opening to the curb, and waved my hand at it. "Come on, kitty. Time to get out. Shoo."

My hand waving had zero effect.

"Kitty cat, you can't sleep here." I gently nudged its rump. It was little more than fur and bone.

The creature fluttered its eyelids at the disturbance, and its head rolled to the side with a scratchy, half-hearted meow.

"You don't look so good. Are you sick?"

I already knew the answer. My parents hadn't allowed pets in our house, but the friend-who-wouldn't-be-named always had one or two at her house. A few times her cats had eaten something that didn't agree with them or ventured into somebody's pesticide-ridden garden and needed a veterinarian's care.

Was that the case with this little one? Either that or simple malnutrition. When I ran my fingers along her back—yes, she was a her—I could feel every dip along her tiny spine and every one of her tiny ribs. I checked her neck.

"No collar or license, huh? Tell you what, you can come home with me tonight, and I'll get you some help tomorrow."

The cat's eyes fluttered again. Her chest rose and fell in a slow, steady rhythm.

"That settles it, then." I closed the passenger side door and made my way back to the driver's seat.

For the rest of the ride, my mind jumped from the ailing kitten behind me, to the emotionally draining discovery of a dead body, to the still-looming task of delivering a bucket-load of bad news to Stirling.

The anxiety was making me so queasy, I wasn't even as happy as I should have been to find an open parking spot in front of my grandfather's apartment building, which occupied the second floor of the building next door to the shop.

Heritage View Apartments consisted of six units above the barbershop and four antique shops that made up the building's street level, along with a lobby entrance for the apartment residents to access their homes. Like my grandfather's shop, a bronze plaque by the awning-covered door dated Heritage View to the early 1900s and declared the apartments to be part of Citrus Grove's rich, historical past.

A fancy way of saying they were old, I guessed.

Old or not, I instantly fell in love with their vintage appeal. The lobby's dark wood molding, coffered ceiling, and marble-tile floor reminded me of something out of an Edith Wharton novel, and if my grandfather's apartment was any indication, the homes were just as elegant.

Although the rooms were small by modern standards, they still had plenty of vintage charm. Stirling's living room, for instance, had a fireplace surrounded by an art nouveau-inspired mantelpiece, period brass wall sconces with fluted glass, and tile work in the bathrooms that would make any art deco lover swoon.

When I'd complimented the old-fashioned features, Stirling told me Heritage View had been the epitome of luxurious living and modern convenience in its heyday.

The place had class to spare, but what it didn't have was a parking lot. It wasn't an issue for Stirling because he didn't own a vehicle. It was a challenge for me, though. I usually had to park a block away in a city lot and walk back. So, when I spotted the open spot near Heritage View's main door, it should have been cause to celebrate.

Tonight, I was too distracted for that. I turned off the

engine and angled back to find my tiny passenger still balled up beneath the seat. "Hey, little one, we're ... here."

I'd nearly said home. But Elk Pass was home. Elk Pass had always been home, and despite everything, I knew I'd eventually go back. I just wasn't ready yet.

I was still getting used to life without my parents and without Mason. That old house and those old rooms didn't feel the same without Mom and Dad. When Stirling had called that first time, it had seemed almost too good to be true. My father had told me his parents had died soon after he graduated high school. I figured there were no pictures or family stories because the memories were so painful. I never questioned it until Stirling Cuthbert called the day after my parents' funeral.

When I asked Stirling why my father hadn't told me about him, he said he and his son had a falling out while my father was in college, and my father had cut all ties. Stirling said he wanted to respect that wish, but when he learned of my parents' passing through a newspaper article, he could no longer remain silent.

I was skeptical at first. A long-lost relative suddenly appearing after a family tragedy sounded like the beginning of a horror movie or a true-crime special.

But there was no money to inherit, and he had no interest in the bookstore or the house, which were all my parents left me.

He only wanted to meet.

Under different circumstances, I would have hesitated, but the truth was, I wasn't handling my parents' loss well. I could barely get myself out of bed to open the store for a few hours a day.

Then, my fiancé—ex-fiancé—decided we weren't a good fit.

After ten years together, that was what he had the nerve to say. "We're not a good fit." Like I was an old coat.

We'd been dating since high school, and I'd waited while he went off to college and law school and through his whole first year at his father's law firm. After our little *Elk Pass Gazette* shut down and I lost my part-time job reporting on our town council, I'd turned down a chance to work at the bigger, regional newspaper because of Mason. He wanted a stay-at-home wife after the wedding, and like an idiot, I'd gone along with it. I'd stayed in Elk Pass, lived with my parents to save money for the wedding, and then, three weeks before our big day, and barely a month after my parents' accident, he dumped me.

Apparently, I wasn't a good fit anymore, but my best friend was. The two of them didn't even try to keep their relationship quiet. Which meant on top of everything else, I had to face the whispers and looks of pity from everyone I knew every time I left the house.

So, I stopped leaving. I stopped going anywhere but the bookstore until I got Stirling's call.

When he invited me to visit him, I didn't think twice. I

threw clothes into a suitcase, locked the door, and drove down the interstate as fast as my trusty blue Subaru could carry me.

I knew then, like I know now, that I can't hide from the pain forever. But, for a little while, I didn't want to think about it.

Any of it.

"Help." It was a soft, childlike voice, little more than a whisper.

I spun around and stared at the kitten, who was still curled up tightly on my floorboard. "Did you hear that?"

The cat opened her glassy, unfocused blue eyes, then closed them again.

Had the plea come from her?

CHAPTER SIX

The Smitten Neighbor

M Y BRAIN WAS playing tricks on me. Of course, it wasn't the cat. Cats didn't talk.

"It's late, I'm tired, and I'm hungry," I said to the tiny bundle of fur. I'd also forgotten to stop at Malone's Diner to pick up dinner. Great.

Going now would mean giving up my parking space, and I didn't feel like walking two blocks from the city lot. I'd rather eat leftovers.

There was also the kitten to consider. I got out of the car and went to the passenger side. When I bent to pick her up, I was prepared for claws, yowls, and squirming, but the little thing was as limp as a wet noodle in my hands. That worried me, so I grabbed the hand towel I kept in the back for emergency spills, folded it to fit in my purse like a makeshift cushion, and laid her on top of it. "There. That should keep you comfortable until we get inside."

The creature hardly stirred as we made our way through the lobby and up the stairs to Stirling's place, which was the first door on the left.

I was so fixated on my little passenger, I lost my grip on the key when I slid it into the lock, and the whole key ring dropped to the floor. As I bent to retrieve it, footsteps rattled the stairs.

"Oh! Pardon me," a woman said when she rounded the corner and nearly collided with me. I'd seen those platinum blond, Marilyn Monroe curls, and the cherry red lips behind the counter at the memorabilia shop next to my grandfather's shop. I'd figured the woman was in her forties, but now that we were face to face, it was clear her heavy makeup was disguising several more years.

"Let me get those for you." The woman scooped up the key ring from the carpet but instead of handing it to me, she pulled it close to her silky red blouse. "I've seen you before. Don't you work at Stirling's store?" Her voice was cheerful, but the sentiment didn't quite make it to her face.

"I do." I smiled brightly and held my purse close to hide the kitten in case Stirling's building had a no-pets policy. The last thing I wanted to do was get him in trouble with his landlord. "Temporarily."

Her lips stretched into a smile, but the rest of her face remained stoic. Had she already seen the kitten? Was she onto me?

"Are you and Stirling related? You must be. You have the same gorgeous green eyes, and I'm told he used to have quite the head of thick, dark hair. Before, you know."

The way she wiggled her fingers at the side of her head to indicate his baldness made me chuckle. There was another strained smile and a hint of a twinkle in her eye.

Maybe I'd misjudged her. Maybe she wasn't suspicious at all. Still, it was better to be safe than sorry, so I kept my purse and the kitten close. "You're right. Stirling is my grandfather. I'm Rebecca."

"How lovely to meet you. I'm Bitsie Baynor. I live two doors down." She pointed one red-lacquered fingernail in the direction of her front door. "I must say, it's nice to see Stirling entertaining. He's such a workaholic, always running off to his shop." She tilted her head to the side. "I've noticed he spends a lot of time alone. May I ask, is he seeing anyone?"

The question caught me by surprise. Was she seriously asking me about my grandfather's love life? I guess at a certain age, there wasn't time or reason to beat around the bush. "Honestly, I don't know."

Some of her twinkle faded.

"But I don't think so," I rushed to add. "He hasn't mentioned anyone."

That shadow of a smile returned. "Good to know. It was nice chatting with you, Rebecca. Please tell your grandfather I said hello." She handed me my keys and turned to make her way to her door.

"Likewise." I pivoted to keep my furry friend out of view. "Nice meeting you."

"And you, dear. Don't forget to tell Stirling."

"I won't." The woman was definitely smitten.

As I closed the door behind myself, I couldn't wait to tell Stirling he had an admirer. Maybe it would cheer him up after I delivered the bad news about Cleopatra's Cat.

But where was he?

In the evenings, he typically sat in his leather recliner by the fireplace and read a book or watched black-and-white movies on TV. Usually, one could find a steaming cup of chamomile tea at his elbow that he nursed for hours.

But the place was dark. His hat was on its hook by the door, which meant he was home, but there was no sign of him. I flipped on a light and noticed his closed bedroom door.

Asleep, I figured, which meant the news about his admirer would have to wait. But it also meant I didn't have to relay the bad news about his broken heirloom or my overnight guest.

"We got lucky," I whispered to the kitten.

My purse passenger didn't stir as I carried her into the guest room and carefully laid her on a pillow on the bed.

Once she was down, her blue eyes opened and glanced around, but then she curled up again and went back to sleep.

Even as scraggly as she was, with her matted fur, coated in flecks of dried leaves and dirt, she was adorable. I ran a fingertip over the fuzz between her ears. "Are you potty trained?"

The odds of that were slim if she was feral. To be safe, I went to my suitcase and pulled out my waterproof windbreaker, folded it, and slipped it beneath her. "This should keep things dry, just in case. Now, how about you stay put while I find something for you to eat."

Before I left, I turned on the small television in the room. It was still paused in the middle of an old episode of *Agatha Christie's Marple*. I'd let the series play as I fell asleep the night before to drown out the building's unfamiliar creaks and moans, as well as the traffic noise from the street below. I hit play again, hoping the TV sounds would drown out any noise my new feline friend might make, at least until I had a chance to tell Stirling why she was here.

That was what I told myself as I scoured the kitchen for something that might interest a cat. The fridge had a jug of orange juice, a few bottled condiments, and four takeout containers. The pantry was a little better. Behind the soup cans, I found a couple cans of tuna. Cats liked tuna, right? Guess I was about to find out.

After searching the drawers for a can opener, I scooped a spoonful of the fish onto a small plate and emptied the rest into a resealable bag I tossed into the fridge before heading back to the room.

When I pushed the plate under her little nose, her eyes shot open. She leaned down to sniff my offering. The bites came slowly at first then with more vigor.

"You're hungry," I mused. "That must be a good sign."

My stomach grumbled as I watched her. "Guess I am, too."

With her occupied, I returned to the kitchen to pick out something from my accumulated leftovers. I grabbed what was left of the strawberry Cobb salad I'd had at Malone's the night before. It was a poor substitute for the spaghetti special, but I grabbed a fork and took it back to the room.

By the time I got there, the kitten's plate was already licked clean, and she was asleep again. She didn't even stir when I settled in beside her to eat and watch the rest of the *Marple* episode.

When I was done, I took my container and the cat's plate back to the kitchen, and washed and dried the dishes.

With that chore done, I checked on the kitten again. She hadn't moved, and no accidents. "Rest up, little one," I whispered as I caressed her head. "We'll get you to a vet in the morning."

She stretched, yawned, and repositioned herself before falling back asleep.

After everything that had happened, I was ready to call it a night, too. I opened my suitcase to get my pajamas.

I was pulling my cupcake-print, fleece pajama top over my head when I heard that strange voice again. Two scratchy, whispered words that sounded like *thank you*.

"Who's there?"

The bedroom door was closed. The window was shut. Was it the TV? It hadn't sounded like the TV.

"Did you hear that?" I glanced at the sleeping kitten.

She didn't respond, not that I expected her to, but I found it reassuring that whatever I'd heard hadn't awakened her. "You're right," I said. "I'm hearing things."

As I pulled on my matching cupcake-print pants and set aside the day's clothes for washing, I ticked through a list of rational explanations. Old pipes. Creaky planks. Outside traffic. Thin walls.

It could have been any one of those. This was a hundred-year-old building with people living next door and a shop below. There were bound to be noises, and considering tonight's grim discovery and two hours of interrogation, who wouldn't be on edge?

The cat stirred and glanced up at me, half-awake. Then she stretched and resumed her slumber.

"You've got the right idea," I whispered. "We both need some shut-eye."

I turned up the television's sound and let Miss Marple's gentle interrogations lull me to sleep.

CHAPTER SEVEN

Brain Tricks

"WAKE UP, MY dear."

Miss Marple leaned over me and brushed a feather across my cheek. It was only a dream, but I didn't care. I pulled the covers over my head to linger in the vision.

"Come now, human. Shake off your slumber."

Human? Even my half-asleep brain knew something was off. Those words were coming from somewhere in this room, not my subconscious. I opened one eye. The television was still on, but the screen had reverted to a bouncing logo. The door was shut, and I was alone, except for the little friend I'd brought home.

Wait, what happened to the cat?

I opened both eyes, rubbed them, and looked again. The matted and disheveled alley creature that had slept on the folded blanket beside my bed was gone. In her place was a fluffy and alert kitten. The grungy, gray fur with black tabby markings was clean and groomed, and she was sitting primly, with her tail wrapped around her paws. She stared at me with bright, sparkling blue eyes.

"Would you be so kind as to provide me with something to eat?"

Had that kitten's mouth moved? Of course not. Cats didn't talk, and they certainly didn't sound like a little Miss Marple. I searched the room again. Someone was having fun at my expense.

Or was I still dreaming? I pinched my wrist. Hard.

"Silly, human. Why did you do that to yourself?"

Okay, still dreaming. This was a dream. I clenched my eyes then opened one of them.

The cat stared at me.

"This isn't funny." I jumped from the bed to check the closet and the bathroom.

The kitten licked her paw and ran it over her head.

The voice that sounded like a miniature version of that British spinster and which might or might not have been coming from that animal said, "I do agree. Perhaps we could discuss the matter over a meal?"

I rubbed my eyes again with my knuckles. "But you're a cat. You can't talk."

When I peeked at her again, those riveting blue eyes were still locked on me.

"Is that so?" said the voice that was definitely and inexplicably coming from that creature.

I sat with that thought for a moment as the kitten continued to lick her paw and groom herself. If I wasn't dreaming and no one else was in the room, what possibilities did that leave? I could think of three. I was hallucinating, I was crazy, or option three, I was both.

Arguing was getting me nowhere, so I tried another approach. "You'll have to forgive me. I'm not used to speaking to a cat."

She glanced up from her paw. "Yet you spoke to me last night."

Had I?

"I was quite weak from the awakening," she continued, "but I heard you. Perhaps it is not the speaking part that troubles you, but the listening part."

Great. This furry figment of my imagination also had an attitude.

"May we return to the matter of sustenance?" she pressed.

I rubbed my forehead. "Will you please fade away or something? I am really not in the mood for this."

She didn't fade. Maybe I should have asked her to morph into something else. George Clooney, perhaps? I'd definitely prefer George Clooney.

"Silly human, I am Aneksi, beloved companion and protector of Queen Cleopatra, the one and true manifestation of our great Mother Isis. If I have risen, she must have need of me. Are you a handmaiden? I demand you take me to her."

That cat was saying a lot of words, but only one of them registered. "Did you say Cleopatra? As in the ruler of ancient

Egypt Cleopatra?"

As I said it, I realized what this was. My subconscious was toying with me. I'd spent the previous night trying to retrieve my grandfather's heirloom statue, a thing that was called Cleopatra's cat.

The epiphany should have broken the spell, but it didn't. The cat was still looking at me and frowning. I swear she was frowning. Then she said, "Ancient? How dare you? My mistress is the one and true ruler of Upper and Lower Egypt, mother to Caesarian, heir to the Roman Empire, and beloved consort to the most honorable and handsome Mark Antony. Take me to her. She must be close. She always keeps me close."

That was it. I grabbed my robe from the hook on the door and pulled it over my pajamas, cupcakes and all. "This is very amusing, but the joke is over. We're done."

I switched off the television and threw open the bedroom door, expecting to find … what exactly? Stirling didn't seem the sort to play pranks, and he was the only other person in the apartment. Still, the possibility of him behaving out of character seemed more believable than the alternative.

"Wait here," I said to the cat, or the hallucination, or whatever it was, and went to the kitchen. I needed caffeine. Luckily, there was one bag left in the box of Scottish breakfast tea.

Once the kettle was filled and heating, I ventured into the living room, where I could see my grandfather's bedroom door was still closed. His fedora was missing from the wall rack by the front door, though, so he must have already gone out. Maybe to grab breakfast at Malone's or to get an early start at the shop.

He must be feeling better if he was up and about, which was a relief. Even more so because I still didn't have to deliver the bad news. A noticeable weight lifted, and I had to wonder. Had that stress caused my imaginary friend? Leave it to my overactive imagination to invent a talking Egyptian cat with a Cleopatra fixation. "Brain tricks," I told myself. "That's what it was."

Feeling lighter and calmer, I ducked back into the galley kitchen.

I wasn't crazy. Stress and probably hunger must have twisted themselves up in my subconscious, and my inner dream factory did the rest.

It made an odd sort of sense. I'd been spending my days surrounded by unusual treasures in the shop then managed to get sucked into Gunther Vernon's homicide investigation. It was too much, and now I was paying the price.

Well, enough with that.

I used the back of a spoon to squeeze every caffeinated drop from the tea bag because it was probably going to be that kind of day. Then I grabbed the leftover tuna from the fridge and dumped it on a plate.

At the bedroom door, with the plate in one hand and my teacup in the other, I paused and shut my eyes. There will not be a talking cat in that room. No. Talking. Cats. I took a deep breath and entered.

The bed was empty, except for the rumpled comforter and my windbreaker, which was still—thankfully—dry.

There were no talking cats. No more hallucinations. I released the breath I'd been holding.

"Here, kitty, kitty, kitty. I brought you food." I crept up to the bed and searched for the gray bundle of fur.

She wasn't there.

Then something moved in the folds of the comforter. I jumped back and splashed hot tea down the front of my robe.

"Oh, my goodness, I do apologize for startling you." Her fluffy gray tail gently thumped the sheets. "Was that for me?"

I set the dishes down on the nightstand and removed the robe. At least nothing had landed on the expensive-looking Persian rug under the bed. As I cleaned the mess, the cat watched with a definite look of amusement.

This isn't real. It. Isn't. Real.

"What happened to the cat I brought home?" Speaking to her as if she knew what I was saying didn't make sense, I knew that. But so far, none of this was making sense.

"Don't be ridiculous, handmaiden. You know very well. It is I, and I am right here." That soft, childlike version of Miss Marple's voice was so sweet and reassuring. She strolled across the bed and hopped gracefully onto the nightstand, where she dipped her nose close to the tuna on the plate. It must have smelled acceptable because she tucked in eagerly.

I dropped down to the floor beside her and watched. "What happened to the little thing that could hardly hold up her own head? You look as strong as an ox."

Her perfectly clean and groomed head lifted. Was that a sneer? "How dare you call me an ox!"

There was that attitude again. I pinched the bridge of my nose. "Like an ox. Not an actual ox."

Still she scowled.

"It's an expression. I'm saying you look healthy."

Her brow furrowed. "I only look like myself. I am Aneksi, beloved companion of—"

"Yes, I know. We've been over that."

She sat back on her haunches and cocked her head to the side. "Tell me, handmaiden, how did I come to be in this place?"

"Don't you remember?"

She closed her eyes and was quiet for a moment. When she opened them, she said, "I was with Mistress Cleopatra in the temple with her priestess. Then I was here, but she is not. Where has she gone?"

"Your mistress? You mean Cleopatra?" What was I saying?

"Yes, Cleopatra." Irritation laced her words.

Before I could answer, her eyes lost focus then she swayed. I grabbed her as she began to tumble over the nightstand's ledge.

Her eyelids fluttered. "Forgive me," she whispered. "I do not feel well." Her head lolled to the side, and a shudder passed through her.

"Are you sick?"

"I feel strange. Exceedingly tired." Her eyes closed, and it was as if her bones had turned to jelly.

I cradled her and feared the worst until that soft, inner motor of hers purred into action. She nuzzled the top of her head against my arm and fell asleep.

Despite her sharp words, she was a sweet little thing. So soft and cuddly and fragile.

"Mistress?" The word rose faintly from her lips, yet it awakened something within me. I barely understood it. Not quite a thought and not quite a feeling, but something deep, primal, and powerful. In that moment, I knew I had to protect her.

"It's not your mistress, Aneksi. It's only me," I whispered. "But I'll take care of you."

And, somehow, I knew she would do the same for me.

CHAPTER EIGHT
Dazed and Distraught

STIRLING WAS AT the desk in the shop's office, examining a tray of turquoise and carnelian pendants. He swiveled around and pushed back his bifocals when he heard me enter. "My dear, I wasn't expecting you so early."

"I wanted to see how you're feeling. Any better?" I dropped my purse on the counter.

"Yes, much better. Just needed a bit of rest. Thank you again for sticking around last night to close up. It was dreadful of me to leave you alone like that."

"It was no trouble. Besides, I was the one nagging you to leave."

He returned his attention to the tray. "Your help is deeply appreciated. But you must let me know if I'm monopolizing your time."

"You're not. I like it here."

That was the truth. Who knew spending my days in a shop filled with such an odd assortment of artifacts and relics—faux and otherwise—could be so satisfying?

Don't get me wrong. I loved my parents' store, with its aisles and aisles of overstuffed bookcases. I would never stop loving books. But the strange treasures in Stirling's shop told stories, too, from the cartouches with their hieroglyphs to the tiny Chinese puzzle boxes to the bronze Hindu gods and goddesses.

Every item evoked a particular spot on the globe and a particular moment in history, whether it was a genuine antique or a replica. I marveled at the jade carvings from China's Song dynasty, and the decorative wooden benches and masks from early Africa, even the jewelry and housewares from the Arabian Peninsula. The Egyptian collection was my favorite, and it took up most of the store.

I could spend hours lingering over the lapis lazuli charms, the terracotta sphinxes and scarabs, and all the figurines of the various gods, goddesses, and pharaohs, imagining the world that created them.

Sometimes, it felt like I'd entered a real-life Adelaide Morris mystery. I could pretend I'd stumbled upon authentic pieces of ancient tombs and temple ruins. It was exciting in a way my own boring life never was.

"Be that as it may," he said, "you haven't even visited any of the beaches yet or Disneyland. You're young. You must want to see the sights."

"There's plenty of time for all that."

"Is there?" His tone told me the question wasn't rhetorical.

I knew what he was trying to say. When I'd accepted his invitation, he'd said I was welcome to stay as long as I liked. He hadn't pressed me for a departure date, and I hadn't offered one. When I left Elk Pass, all I could think about was getting away. Even now, more than a week later, I felt no urgency to get back.

"There is," I said. "Would you mind if I made myself a cup of tea?"

"Of course. You needn't ask," he said. "Consider the shop and the apartment your own for as long as you wish it. However long that may be."

The offer sounded genuine. Maybe I had read too much into his gently probing questions. Or maybe I was overthinking and overanalyzing, as I had a tendency to do.

"Thank you." The words sounded so inadequate for how grateful I was, but I couldn't think of anything else that wasn't overly sentimental. Although he was family, we were still getting to know each other.

It also didn't feel like the right time to deliver a depressing load of bad news, either. *Hey, thanks for everything you're doing for me, but you know that stolen cat statue you were hoping to get back? Well, that's not going to happen. It's destroyed. Sorry.*

Ugh.

I'd have to find a way to tell him soon, though. While I considered the possibilities, I went to the counter where the electric kettle was plugged in. "Can I make you a cup, too?"

"I wouldn't turn down some Earl Grey."

As I filled the kettle from the bottled water beside it, I considered my other pressing concern. How should I tell him about the kitten? Before leaving, I'd moved her to the bathroom, which would be easier to clean than the guest room when nature eventually called. I also made sure she had a comfy blanket, a bowl of water, and more tuna.

Since she was sleeping when I left, I hoped she'd continue to sleep. Still, I couldn't leave her alone for long, even if she did seem so much better than she had the night before. I wanted to bring her to the shop, but I needed Stirling's permission first.

"How do you feel about cats?" The question slipped out before I'd completely thought it through, and I winced at how obvious it sounded.

"Real cats? Or cats as they were depicted by the ancients?"

"Real cats."

"Can't stand them, to be honest. Miserable creatures." He made a grunting, shuddering sort of noise for emphasis. "Why do you ask?"

So much for my plan. "No reason." Heat crept up my neck to my cheeks. Was it me, or was it getting hot in here? The room didn't have a window, but there was a vent in the wall above my head. I waved my hand over it, searching for a cooler breeze.

"The vent doesn't work, if that's what you're wondering," Stirling said. "We tried to install air-conditioning a few years ago, but the town's historical preservation commission put a stop to it. It would alter the original character of the building, they said. Never mind the original building was a bank that was carved up into separate units in the 1920s. Apparently, that's fine, but when it comes to a little modern comfort, that's a bridge too far. There's an electric fan in the storage room, if you need it."

I'd obviously triggered a sore spot.

"Is that the turquoise shipment you were expecting?" I turned my attention, and I hoped his, back to the pendants scattered on the velvet-covered tray on his desk.

"Oh, these?" He pulled them closer and arranged the stones more neatly. "Yes, they arrived this morning from my agent in Luxor. He's included quite a few carnelian pieces as well. Marvelous specimens. Just marvelous."

When I finished filling the kettle and set it on the heat element, I peered over his shoulder. "They're beautiful. Are they Egyptian?"

He lowered the black magnifying monocle he'd attached to his bifocals and peered at them. "They certainly are. I think I'll display them near the register. They'll be popular with the tourist crowd, I think."

The kettle whistled, so I switched it off and pulled two cups from the cupboard and filled them with tea bags— Scottish breakfast for me, Earl Grey for him—before pouring the just-shy-of-boiling water over them. It was the way my father had taught me to prepare tea, and it had earned me an approving nod from Stirling the first time I prepared his. I wondered if he'd taught my father that technique, but I hadn't yet mustered the courage to ask.

I handed him his cup. "Should we open?"

He pulled up his pocket watch. "Yes, yes. Time has gotten away from me." He pushed back the jewelry tray and adjusted the yellow silk bow tie that sat atop his pecan brown sweater vest like a little ray of sunshine.

As I went to the front door, he followed me. "I fell asleep so early last night, I didn't hear you come in. I hope you didn't have any trouble closing up."

This was my chance. I had to tell him I'd left early and, more importantly, why. But, oh, I was dreading it. "There was no trouble with the closing, but a man called about that stolen figurine you told me about."

His face brightened. "Cleopatra's cat? Someone knows where it is?"

"Sort of. His name was Gunther Vernon. Do you know him?"

Those plunging eyebrows indicated he did but not in a good way. "I'm familiar with him," he said. "He has it?"

I flipped the closed sign to open and lingered at the window, wishing I could skip past the delivering-bad-news part of the conversation and get right to the consoling and look-for-the-silver-lining part.

"I suppose so," I said carefully. "He wanted you to go to

his house so he could return it, but I didn't want to disturb you, so I went. I closed the shop a few minutes early." The guilt was making me rush my words. "I wanted to surprise you, but when I got to his house…" A knot formed in my chest. I bit my lip, hoping it would pass.

My grandfather moved closer. "My dear, was he inappropriate with you? I wish you would have told me. I never would have let you go there, especially on your own. Gunther Vernon is a despicable man."

"Not anymore."

Stirling's concern turned to confusion. "He wasn't despicable?"

"Actually, he's dead."

My grandfather stumbled forward before catching himself. "Dead? But how? Oh! Did he … I mean, did you…"

"No, it wasn't me. He was dead when I found him. It looked like he had been attacked. That's what the police said."

"The police were there?"

"I called 911 when I found him. You wouldn't believe how many police cars showed up. I lost count at eight, not to mention the vans for the CSI people and the coroner."

Stirling listened and nodded. When I was done explaining the whole grisly scene, he clasped his hands in front of himself. "But you were able to retrieve Cleopatra's cat?"

The cringe started in my toes and worked its way to every other extremity. "I tried, but…"

He leaned closer. "But?"

"It was broken. Pieces were scattered across the floor of his study."

Watching Stirling absorb the fact that his treasured heirloom was destroyed was almost more than I could bear.

"It broke?" he said quietly.

"I'm so, so sorry. I know it meant a lot to you."

Those wide-open eyes stared at me, but they weren't seeing me anymore. They weren't seeing anything. I wanted to say something reassuring or sympathetic, but what? How could I possibly know what it felt like to have something so precious destroyed? So, I changed the subject.

"My tea needs more sugar. How about yours?" I hurried past him and slipped back into the office. I scooped a half-teaspoon of the raw stuff into my cup and stirred.

The bell on the front door jingled, letting us know someone had entered the shop.

Stirling had followed me back into the office with that dazed and distraught look in his eyes.

"I'll take care of the customer," I said. "You drink your tea." I wanted to be helpful, since there was little else I could do, but when I saw who had crossed the threshold, I nearly backtracked.

Unfortunately, Detective Devon, looking official in his jacket and tie, had already seen me. He glared my direction as he pulled a pen from an inside pocket. "Miss Rebecca Cuthbert. Exactly the person I was hoping to see. Did you forget our appointment?"

My hands flew to my mouth. I tried to smile to hide my embarrassment. "Good morning, detective. You're not going to believe this, but that's exactly what happened."

He feigned surprise. "Should I be insulted? Did I make so little of an impression on you last night?"

Stirling emerged from the office and stood beside me. "What's going on here? Do you have business with my granddaughter?" He placed a protective hand on my shoulder.

"Good morning, Mr. Cuthbert. I need to speak to Rebecca about a situation last night. I don't know if she's explained that she was involved in a homicide."

"That's preposterous! She didn't even know the man."

"That's what she says, but she was inside his house."

"I told you the door was open," I wailed.

The detective smirked and shook his head. "The housekeeper says that door is always locked, and considering the valuables Mr. Vernon keeps inside, I'm inclined to believe her. Which means—"

"Which means you don't believe me." I could see where this was going, and I didn't like it.

"Which *means*," he continued with emphasis, "that I'm wondering if you've been completely honest with me."

"Now see here, detective." Stirling's face was getting redder by the second. "I will not have you bullying her. You are completely out of line."

"Sir, a man was murdered last night, and I intend to find his killer. That means I am going to ask Miss Cuthbert some questions, and since she wasn't willing to come to the station on her own, I can only assume she has something to hide."

"What? I don't have anything to hide. I told you it was a mistake." Did this guy honestly think I was responsible for Gunther Vernon's death? My heart was beating so hard in my chest, I thought I was having a heart attack. "I swear, I just forgot."

Detective Devon reached behind his back and fished something out of his back pocket. "Here's something I doubt you'll forget." He produced a shiny pair of silver handcuffs and walked toward me. "Rebecca Cuthbert, you are under arrest."

CHAPTER NINE
Police Station

DETECTIVE DEVON LED me out of the shop to a black-and-white squad car double parked in front of the Golden Oldies Memorabilia Shoppe next door.

Just my luck. My friendly neighbor, Bitsie Baynor, was changing her window display as we walked by. Actually, she was watching us and pretending to change her window display. I could only imagine what she was thinking.

Scratch that. I knew exactly what she was thinking.

My stomach lurched as we approached the vehicle. "You aren't really going to make me get in there, are you?"

He nudged me toward the rear passenger door. "You should be grateful I put the handcuffs away. Any more complaints, and I might pull them out again."

To my relief, he'd backed off his threat to arrest me as soon as I agreed to accompany him to the station.

"I'm not complaining." I was, but I really didn't like the look of those cuffs. "My car's parked around the corner. If you give me directions, I can meet you there. Then you won't have to bring me back afterward. It'll be easier for you."

He chuckled, revealing a dimple in his left cheek. If he wasn't so annoying, he might actually be cute. I even sort of liked the way he always smelled like an open box of cinnamon candy.

"Easier for me, huh? I doubt that." He didn't even try to disguise the sarcasm as he opened the car door and motioned for me to get in.

A snide comment would have put him in his place, but I didn't want those handcuffs to reappear. Especially when the neighbors were watching. "You made your point. I shouldn't have forgotten our meeting. But in my defense, I had other things going on."

He scratched his freshly shaved chin. "You must lead quite an interesting life if a murder investigation slips your mind so easily."

"It didn't slip my mind. Okay, it did, but you'd be distracted, too, if a sad little stray cat found its way into your car." I was making a presumption, but who wouldn't be distracted by a furry kitten? "She seemed sick, so I took her home to feed her." I left it at that. No point sharing the embarrassing details of my weird hallucinations.

I glanced back at Cuthbert Exotic Antiques to be sure Stirling was still inside. It wasn't how I wanted him to learn I'd brought a stray into his home without permission. But now he was rearranging his window display and pretending not to watch me and the detective. Maybe he and Bitsie were made for each other.

"So, you're an angel of mercy, huh? That's why you're too busy to do your civic duty?"

Great. More sarcasm. Forget the dimple and the cinnamon sweetness. This guy was plain annoying.

"I wasn't too busy, I forgot. Big difference."

"Right. Big difference."

He slid behind the steering wheel, started the vehicle, and maneuvered us into traffic. I ignored him and kept track of the route, in case I had to find my own way back.

"Comfortable back there?"

He had to be kidding. I was sitting on hard, contoured plastic, not a cushion. I knocked on it. "Are the seats so uncomfortable on purpose?"

I caught a glimmer of Detective Scowls-a-Lot's amusement in the rearview mirror.

"They aren't designed for comfort," he said. "They're designed to keep the occupants safe and us safe. They also have to be easy to clean, for obvious reasons."

"What reasons?"

There was that dimple again. "Think about it. Drug addicts? Drunk and disorderlies? Our clientele isn't known for having the best control of their faculties, if you know what I mean."

As the meaning dawned on me, I pulled my hands into my lap and tried to shrink into the smallest possible space.

"All that happens back here?"

"It has on occasion. You feeling okay?" That single eyebrow hiked skyward.

"Fine, thank you. Are we almost there?" Had I really said that? "Sorry. I haven't said those words in twenty years. It used to drive my mom nuts." I could almost see her in the driver's seat of our old station wagon, telling me for the umpteenth time that we'd get there when we got there.

The memory unleashed a fresh flood of emotion, and I missed her and Dad all over again.

It took a few deep breaths to compose myself, and once I did, I glanced up to find the detective still watching me in the mirror.

"Something wrong?" he asked.

"I lost my parents recently." The words spilled out before I could stop them, and I regretted them instantly. I tried to lighten the mood. "It just hits me at the oddest times. Like now, apparently." I tried to chuckle, but it sounded more like a strangled weasel. I winced. "Sorry, that's more than you probably wanted to know. Don't mind me. I'll just be back here, keeping my mouth shut." Seriously, I had to stop talking.

I stared at my lap so I wouldn't see him watching me through the mirror, but I could feel it like a blowtorch on my skin. Why was I rambling like an idiot?

"I'm sorry," he said softly. "That couldn't have been easy. But we're here, if that's any consolation."

From the passenger window, I watched him swerve into a parking lot enclosed by a concrete block wall. He stopped at the guard booth and flashed his badge. The attendant waved him through.

"This is it?"

I must have sounded disappointed because he laughed. "Not what you were expecting?"

"I don't know what I was expecting, but this wasn't it." This was two stories of brown stucco that could have housed anything. An insurance company, a medical office, maybe a bank. I suppose all the police cars in the lot gave it away, though. There were dozens of them, lined up in long, tidy rows.

"What's the station in Elk Pass look like?"

"We don't have one. We have two part-time sheriff's deputies who work out of their cars, mostly. They have a desk and a phone in the post office, if they need it. If they need to take someone to jail, it's a twenty-minute drive to the county building. That doesn't happen much, though."

"Must be a nice place." He pulled the car into an empty spot and killed the engine.

"It is." At least it had been.

"After we sort out the investigation, maybe you can get back there." He stepped out of the car and came around to open my door, since there was no way to open it from the inside.

I glared up at him. "*Maybe* I'll be able to get back there?

What does that mean? You said I wouldn't be arrested if I cooperated and, here I am, cooperating."

"Right, and I haven't arrested you. But if the investigation implicates you or if you try to skip town before the investigation ends, that'll change things. Will you come inside and finish that interview now, or are you going to sit there and make my job more difficult?"

The man was infuriating. I got out of the car and smoothed the white, button-down shirt I'd worn with my jeans. "Please, lead the way."

He rolled his eyes. "You really can't help yourself, can you?"

I ignored the question. All I wanted to do was get this over with so I could get away from him. I gritted my teeth. "After you, detective."

He ushered me through the automatic, double glass doors to a wide expanse of linoleum that ended at a wood-paneled counter and thick acrylic windows that protected two clerks from the lines of people waiting to speak with them.

We pushed through a low swinging door to the back area, where metal desks were pushed together in various formations. The cacophony of ringing phones and a dozen conversations going at once made my head hurt, and the reek of stale coffee didn't help.

He led me down another corridor, then through another open room of desks and offices. "You're taking me to one of those dreary interrogation rooms with the two-way mirrors, aren't you? That's where the TV cops always take the criminals."

"Are you saying you're a criminal?"

Was that a joke? I hoped so. "I might as well be. You're treating me like one."

He shook his head. "You are dead set on making this as difficult as possible, aren't you?"

The hallway opened to yet another room. This one had gray cubicles, which was a modest improvement from the bare metal desks. He turned down an aisle, then another, before gesturing to a chair pulled up at the end of a desk. He removed his jacket and hung it from a hook. "Take a seat. Can I get you some coffee?"

"Yes." It didn't matter that I'd just had tea. I wasn't going to pass up a chance for real coffee.

He stepped away without asking how I took it, which worried me until he came back and dropped a small pile of colorful packets—white for the powdered creamer; pink, blue, yellow, white, and brown for the sweeteners—on his desk beside two small cups of steaming coffee. I waited as he took four creamer containers before I dove in for the two raw sugar packets.

"So, this is where you work?" I asked before taking a sip.

It was a good thing he turned around to tap the name plate stuck to his cubicle wall, which read, DET. NICK DEVON, because it took every ounce of self-control not to spray that acid wash across the pile of folders stacked on his desk. Once I swallowed, I set the cup down and pushed it as far away as I possibly could.

When Detective Devon turned back around, he looked at me and frowned. "What's wrong now? Has something else about the Citrus Grove Police Department fallen below your lofty expectations?"

This wasn't the time to discuss the crime that was that cup of coffee. "No. I mean, it's nice." Nice? Boy, I was on a roll.

"Let me guess. You were expecting someplace grittier, something like you see on *Law & Order*?"

"No." But, yes, that was exactly what I was expecting. I'd never admit it to him, though.

"You watch too much television," he mumbled as he took a folder from the pile on his desk and opened it, revealing stacks of pages pinned to both inside covers, before opening a drawer and pulling out a ballpoint pen.

Before he closed the drawer, I caught sight of a dozen boxes of red cinnamon candies stacked in there. No wonder he smelled like an autumn candle.

He scribbled a note on the file's top sheet. "You said you weren't previously acquainted with Gunther Vernon."

"Right. I've never met him."

Then he repeated the same questions he had asked me the day before.

"Is there a reason you're making me tell you this again? It

seems like a huge waste of time for both of us. Shouldn't you be looking for the killer?"

"I am looking for the killer, Miss Cuthbert." That scowl of his turned my knees to jelly, but not in the good way. "I'm having trouble understanding how you happened to be in the house, looking for your stolen merchandise, at the exact same time Mr. Vernon came to his untimely end. Especially when you had motive and opportunity."

Was this a joke? Did he honestly think I was capable of killing that man? "But I'm the one who called you."

He rubbed his lower lip as he stared at another page in the file. "Could be a clever way to try to throw suspicion off yourself."

"That doesn't make sense at all." But actually, it did make a terrible, twisted kind of sense, if one was a terrible and twisted kind of person. But I wasn't. Why couldn't he see that? "I'm not a killer. I'm just a woman trying to help her grandfather."

He leaned back in his chair and folded his arms. "So you've said. You know, I took the liberty of calling the Elk Pass sheriff's station. They have quite an interesting file on you. Nothing of note until about a month ago. Then there's public intoxication, a petty theft, and"—he flipped a few sheets in the folder—"oh yes, assault with a deadly weapon."

I buried my head in my hands. "That was one night. One awful, horrible night."

"I should say so." His eyes weren't on the form anymore.

They were on me.

"I was a mess, okay? It was after my parents died and before what was supposed to be my wedding, and out of the blue, my fiancé tells me he's in love with my best friend. Honestly, I probably would have been fine if the wedding champagne hadn't been delivered to my house. That whole night is kind of a blur. I don't even remember most of the things the deputy said I did."

"Like putting a guy in the hospital?"

"It wasn't a guy. It was Mason. My ex-fiancé. The doctor said it was just a broken nose. He suffered worse on the football field in high school."

"And the slashed truck tires?"

"Mason's truck. But in my defense, he was parked at Lacey's house. That's my best friend. Was my best friend." This whole trip down memory lane was making me queasy.

"I think I get the picture." He flipped the page back down.

"I did not kill Gunther Vernon. I would never do that."

He nodded. "Yet there's still the problem of you saying you'd never been to Mr. Vernon's house before."

"Why is that a problem?"

He scowled again. "Ms. Henriksen told us she saw you there two days ago, when you delivered the cat statue we found in pieces on the floor."

"She said what?"

He repeated it, but it still didn't make sense. "She's lying.

I didn't do that."

He shook his head. "You've said that item was stolen from your grandfather, but it seems possible that you were the one who stole it."

This was getting worse by the second. "Why would I do that? Besides, it was stolen before I even got to town. I told you that."

"I did some checking after you mentioned the theft at Cuthbert Exotic Antiques."

"Then you know Martin Fincher took it. Check the police report."

He rubbed his chin. "See, that's the thing. There isn't a police report. There's no record of a theft involving Cuthbert Exotic Antiques at all. Are you sure you're not mistaken?"

These Citrus Grove cops were the worst. "No, I'm not mistaken. Ask my grandfather."

As I grew more heated, he became calmer. "I will," he said flatly.

Was he serious? Was he patronizing me? I couldn't tell.

He rubbed his chin. "Ms. Henriksen is a compelling witness."

"But she's lying." How many times did I have to say that?

The twist of his lips told me he still wasn't convinced.

"She has no reason to lie."

"How do you know that? You're the detective. There must be a reason."

He sank back in his chair again and stared at me.

And stared.

I clasped my hands in my lap and stared back at him. "Are we done with the questions yet?"

His eyes narrowed. "I guess we are. For now."

"Great. Will you take me back to the shop?"

He grabbed the phone receiver on his desk and punched a button. "My guest needs a ride to the circle," he said. "The sooner the better."

He hung up, scooped up the investigation file, and stood.

I rose too.

He held up his hand to stop me. "You can wait here. Someone will be by in a minute to take you back. I appreciate your time, Miss Cuthbert. Have a pleasant day."

As he walked away, my hopes surged. He hadn't arrested me, and I was free to go. But I couldn't shake the feeling that this wasn't over. "Are we done, then?"

The detective stopped and looked back. "I still have plenty of questions. But don't worry. I'm sure we'll have the answers we need soon enough."

That should have put me at ease. So, why was there still a hot ball of flaming anxiety churning in my stomach?

CHAPTER TEN

Malone's Diner

THE UNIFORMED OFFICER buckled his seatbelt and glanced back at me through the squad car's rearview mirror. "You don't remember me, do you, Miss Cuthbert?"

I'd recognized the officer's wavy, sun-bleached hair and that ruddy tan the instant he approached Detective Devon's desk, but I was still stewing over the insinuation that I could be Gunther Vernon's killer.

The officer must have interpreted my silence as confusion because he tried to help me out. "We met at the murder, uh, I mean the Vernon house. I was helping Detective Devon."

I pretended to suddenly remember. "That's right. Officer Meadows. You were interviewing the housekeeper."

He raised his finger to stop me.

"Sorry," I rushed to say. "I meant domestic manager."

The corners of his blue eyes crinkled. "It's a mistake I'll never make again. She really let me have it. Not that she didn't have a right to. I respect a woman who takes pride in her job."

"That's a nice way of looking at it." I suppose I'd be impressed, too, if she hadn't told the detective I was the one who delivered Cleopatra's cat to Gunther. Thanks to her, the detective thought I was a suspect.

Why would she do it?

A possible answer struck me like a lightning bolt. Maybe she was the killer.

That scenario played out in my mind. Eva Henriksen, who couldn't have been more than five foot in her stocking feet, fighting with Gunther Vernon, who was several inches taller. The mental image was almost comical, and if I had been in a better frame of mind, I might have laughed. It was difficult to see how she could ever overpower a man like Gunther.

Which brought me back to my original question, why would she lie about me?

The thought sat at the back of my mind as the eucalyptus and palm trees passed outside my window. What I needed was someone like Adelaide Morris, someone who could step in when the police were on the wrong track.

If only there were a real Adelaide Morris, and not just a literary heroine whose investigations were limited to the pages of her mystery novels. I needed somebody who was as clever and fearless as she was. Someone who could find the truth among the lies as easily as she found treasures in the long-buried tombs of the ancient pharaohs.

She was an unlikely detective, yet with her signature perseverance and grit, she always prevailed. "A murder investigation is not so different from an excavation," she'd quipped in one of her novels. "One must follow the clues with patience and tenacity until they reveal their secrets." She made it sound so easy.

Was it?

I had read every one of her books multiple times and knew each one of her investigations inside and out. It wasn't the same as real-world experience, obviously. But it was experience, wasn't it? Besides, it wasn't like I was getting any help from the detective, so what did I have to lose?

"Isn't it a shame about Ms. Henriksen's condition?" I asked, trying to mimic Adelaide Morris's habit of asking casual but relevant questions, as Officer Meadows maneuvered through traffic.

His frown reflected back at me in the rearview mirror. "What do you mean? What's her condition?"

"Oh, I thought it was obvious when she lost her temper with you. People in the early stages of dementia often struggle to control their emotions."

I had no idea if that was true, but I'd read something to that effect once and it had stuck with me. What I really wanted to do was get him talking about why that woman might say something blatantly false.

"That hadn't occurred to me," he said. "I figured she just had a mean streak. You'd be surprised how many people scream at us, even the ones we're trying to help."

"That must be frustrating. I guess I assumed it must be something medical after Detective Scowls … uh, Devon told me what she'd said about seeing me at the house before yesterday. I mean, that absolutely didn't happen, so why would she lie about it?"

The officer frowned. "I really couldn't say. But, uh, is that what he said?"

Was he onto me? He stiffened, and his eyebrows did an awkward little dance.

I backpedaled. "That's what he said. Crazy, right?"

The officer's response? A slight tip of the head then nothing. He stared straight ahead.

So much for my investigative skills. He wasn't going to tell me anything helpful now.

But I couldn't give up. My life, or at least my freedom, depended on it.

If I couldn't coax him into telling me something to prove her accusation was false, I needed to find another way. Something that would lead to the real killer. Something that would…

As Malone's Diner passed by, its blazing red neon sign hooked my attention. The sign was the same color and design as the logo on the takeout bags, like the one I'd seen on Gunther Vernon's desk.

Gunther had either been to the restaurant or had an order delivered shortly before his death, which meant somebody at Malone's might have been the last person to see him alive, and maybe he hadn't been alone.

It was a long shot, but it was the only shot I had. Besides, I'd built up an appetite answering the detective's questions, and an order of eggs and bacon sounded really good. I leaned forward. "Instead of taking me to the shop, could you drop me off at Malone's?"

We were already in the traffic circle, but Officer Meadows shrugged. "Sure." He tilted his wrist to read his watch. "Probably smart. Get in before the lunch crowd and before Hank hands the grill over to one of the lunch cooks. His cooks are great, don't get me wrong, but Hank Malone is a master. Just like his dad."

He seemed more cheerful now that we'd changed subjects, and certainly more talkative, but honestly, I'd never noticed who was behind the grill when Stirling and I ate there. "So, Hank is the Malone in Malone's Diner?" I asked.

"He is now, but his great-grandfather opened the place. It's one of the oldest businesses on the circle. Kinda like your grandfather's shop."

The officer slid into a parking spot on the street, put the transmission in park, and jumped out to open my door.

"If you haven't tried the custard French toast yet, I highly recommend it." He chef-kissed the air. "It's totally awesome."

"Thanks. Maybe I will. And thanks for the ride." I grabbed my purse by the strap and held it at arm's length until I could give it a thorough scrub. No telling what it picked up in the back of that car.

The officer closed the door behind me. "Happy to be of service. See you around." He slid back behind the wheel.

As I smiled and waved, I secretly hoped I wouldn't see him or anyone from the police department any time soon. I kept up the wave, though, as he drove away, in case anyone inside was watching. If anyone was watching, I hoped they'd think the ride was a friendly gesture, not a prelude to an arrest. Considering this morning's spectacle, I already had some explaining to do with Stirling's smitten neighbor.

As I stood on the sidewalk, smelling the deliciousness wafting from the diner, my stomach reminded me I was hungry, and that custard French toast did sound tasty. I ducked inside and saw a guy with long sideburns sitting at one of the lunch counter's red vinyl stools, sipping coffee and thumbing through a newspaper. A couple of the high-back booths were occupied, but all the vintage Formica and chrome tables were empty. The place was dead.

Hank Malone spotted me through the kitchen's pass-through window. "Hey, Rebecca." He squeezed his eyes shut, then popped them open. "Cheese omelet with bacon on the side, right?"

Stirling had introduced me to Hank when he waited on our table for breakfast a few days ago, but the place had been too busy for him to stop and chat. That he'd remembered my name and my order was impressive. Maybe Officer

Meadows was right, running a diner was in this guy's blood.

"Good memory!" I called back. "But today, I think I'd like to try the custard French toast. Make that two orders, plus a side of plain tuna?"

He gave me a funny look, and I felt compelled to explain one of the orders was for Stirling and the tuna was for a cat, but I stopped myself. I couldn't get sidetracked, not when my future was at stake. I took a deep breath and reminded myself to do what Adelaide would do. "Do you know Gunther Vernon?"

His head popped up. "The guy who was murdered?"

My hopes lifted. "Yeah, did you see him in here yesterday? Maybe late in the afternoon?"

He looked away. "No. He wasn't here."

"Are you sure? He's in sixties, I think. Tall. Athletic build. Short, silver hair." Blue lips. Blood pooling around the ears. I kept those details to myself.

Hank grimaced and shook his head.

Maybe the order would trigger a memory. "He ordered a cheeseburger with fries. With a medium-sized drink. Cola, I think."

Hank shrugged, half distracted by something on the griddle. "Sorry. You've described about half of my customers."

As I racked my brain for more defining characteristics, something that would narrow the field, someone stepped up behind me.

"Rebecca, what a lovely surprise!"

I whipped around to find Bitsie Baynor with her perfectly curled hair and perfectly painted red lips tugged into a tight smile.

"Did I hear you mention Gunther Vernon?" she asked.

"I did. I think he was either here or had an order delivered to his home yesterday before…"

She nodded solemnly, letting me know she understood.

"Do you know him?" I asked.

Instead of answering, she looked past me to the kitchen pass-through. "Unfortunately, we do, don't we, Hank?"

When I looked at him, Hank's cheeks had flushed red. I was still no Adelaide Morris, but I knew a man caught in a lie when I saw one.

CHAPTER ELEVEN
Collision

"GUNTHER USED TO come into Malone's quite a bit," Bitsie said in her serene manner. "But I haven't seen him here in weeks. Have you, Hank?"

His face was still a deep crimson. "The guy used to come in, but not for a while. He wasn't in yesterday, but he might have used a meal delivery service. Lots of people do."

"Is it possible the driver saw someone in the house with Gunther when he made the delivery?" My long shot was turning into an impossible shot, but there was no harm in asking.

"I wouldn't know," Hank said. "Those meal delivery guys come in and pick up the bags. We don't know where the food goes after it leaves here."

That was unfortunate. "Maybe I could talk to the delivery person?"

"We see some of the same faces," he said, "but we work with five different services, and they each employ dozens of drivers who work all over the area. If you want to hang around, you might see a few of them, but I'm not sure that would be much help. Do you have the receipt?"

I shook my head.

"If you had that, it might be easier to track down the driver. Without it, I don't have a clue how you'd figure it out. Sorry."

"Okay, thanks." I tried to hide my disappointment, but I must not have been doing a good job of it because Bitsie patted my shoulder.

"Why are you interested in Gunther's food order?" she asked. "Is it part of the police investigation?"

"No, I guess not. I just thought it might be relevant."

"Brandt didn't say something?" she pressed.

"Brandt?" I repeated.

"Brandt Meadows," she clarified. "I saw him drop you off outside."

This woman didn't miss a thing, did she? Whatever she thought about my personal police escort remained hidden behind that placid expression.

"Right. Yes. Officer Meadows. He was driving me back from the station. They had some questions about what happened." I hoped she'd think I was a witness, not a suspect.

"Relating to Gunther's homicide?" she added.

"Yes, exactly." I really wanted to change the subject, but my mind went completely blank.

Luckily, she stepped in to save me from the awkward silence. "They must have sworn you to secrecy. That's how those things work, isn't it?"

"It is," I said, still racking my brain for a new topic.

Bitsie hardly seemed to notice. She was motioning to a young woman with a shroud of wild, tawny curls sitting at a rear booth. "Luna, darling, come meet Stirling's granddaughter. She's delightful."

My cheeks burned. I didn't feel delightful. Discouraged was more like it, since my attempt at an investigation had already failed miserably.

Still, I struggled to smile for the willowy woman who had gathered her things and was approaching us. In her breezy, botanical print dress that brushed her bare ankles and the tops of her leather sandals, she looked like she should be strolling through a sunny garden or along the shoreline, not navigating between empty diner chairs.

"Okay, two custard French toasts and a side of tuna. Can I get you anything else?"

A spray tan? A stomach I didn't have to suck in to get my jeans zipped up? Hair I didn't have to wrestle into a messy bun every morning? But then, that probably wasn't what he meant.

"Can I get a coffee to go?" If a makeover wasn't in the cards, I could at least walk out of here with a decent cup of coffee.

"Sure thing." He pulled a tall paper cup from beneath the counter and took it to the machine.

As I waited, Miss Supermodel joined Bitsie. She put out her hand with the friendliest of smiles. "Hi, Rebecca. I'm Luna Sage."

Wouldn't you know it? She was friendly, too. Life really wasn't fair. "Nice to meet you," I replied with a quick handshake.

The older woman laid a motherly hand on her companion's shoulder. "Luna is the Golden Oldies' shop manager, and she's been such a blessing. One silver lining, I suppose, to that terrible business with Martin."

That name shook me. "Do you mean Martin Fincher?"

Something like panic crossed Luna's face, but Bitsie only sighed and nodded. "I've gone over it in my mind a thousand times. How could I not have seen it? I will never forgive him for what he did to your grandfather, but I'm still grateful that he steered dear Luna my way. I have to give him credit for that."

"I'll give him something else, if he ever shows his face around here again."

I spun around at Hank's threat. His earlier sheepishness was gone, replaced by something far more menacing. His hands formed tight fists on the counter, making his knuckles turn white.

"I'm sure we've seen the last of Martin," Luna added quickly as she moved closer to the counter and to Hank. She covered one of his hands with her own in a soft, sweet gesture.

He grumbled, "I hope you're right." Then he slid the bag and a to-go cup of coffee toward me and rang up my order on the cash register.

I took a sip as I waited, but as soon as it hit my tongue, I winced and tried not to spit it back out. So much for a decent cup of coffee. I wasn't giving up, though. I grabbed several sugar packets and dropped them into the bag while Hank finished ringing me up.

When I handed him a few bills to pay for my order, he tucked them into the register's tray and returned my change. But it was too much.

I handed him back a few dollars. "I think you made a mistake. I still owe you this."

He pushed in the cash drawer and put up his hands. "No mistake. It's the locals' discount."

"But I'm not a local."

"Stirling is," he countered. "He's as local as they come. We can call it a family discount, if it makes you feel better."

That rough exterior was gone, and he was cheerful Hank once again. "Thank you," I said. "It's generous of you." I tucked the bills back into my purse, trying carefully to touch as little of the exterior as possible until I could douse it in sanitizer.

"It is generous," Bitsie interjected. "But don't let him fool you. He knows how to keep us coming back. Don't you, Hank?"

"Just being neighborly. Want me to put that in a to-go

cup for you?" He gestured at Bitsie's coffee cup, and she handed it to him.

That was the perfect description of this place. Neighborly. As much as the people around here talked about the town's historic buildings and vintage charm, there was something special about its old-fashioned friendliness too. Bitsie didn't have to come to my rescue, but she did. Hank didn't have to forgive me for my clumsy questions, but he did.

I was still thinking about that as I made my way to the door and saw the spaghetti and meatballs sign sitting beside it. I turned back. "I know I shouldn't be thinking about dinner yet, but you wouldn't happen to have any of last night's special left over, do you? I meant to come by, but my night went sideways. Spaghetti was my mom's specialty, and it's always been one of my favorites."

"Is that so?" Bitsie seemed overly interested. "Did you know Hank is now selling his mother's original recipe? He cans it himself, right here in the restaurant."

"I didn't know that," I said. "It's a great idea. The stuff you get at the store never matches a really good homemade sauce."

Hank beamed. "That's what Bitsie said. I have to give her credit for the idea."

Bitsie held her hand to her mouth and pretended to whisper. "All I did was tell him it was so good, he should bottle it. He's going to make a fortune, too, which will come in handy, won't it?"

His smile disappeared. "I suppose it will." His glance slid back to Luna. "Luna came up with a great label design, and I found some nice jars. Bitsie, you haven't even seen the final product yet. Come on back, and I'll show you."

Bitsie and Luna followed him when he disappeared through the kitchen's swinging doors.

I had already stuck around longer than I intended, so I headed for the exit. With the bag of food in one hand and my cup of coffee in the other, I backed into the swinging door to open it. When I was halfway through, I turned to walk out, but a petite, white-haired woman tapping on her phone's screen slammed into me, sending my hot coffee tumbling to the ground. Not before it drenched my sleeve, though.

"Oh," the woman exclaimed when she glanced up from her phone. "It's you!"

Standing in front of me without a hint of remorse was Eva Henriksen.

CHAPTER TWELVE
Cleanup Crew

"I'M SO SORRY, Ms. Henriksen." I apologized, even though she had obviously rammed into me. Still, my mother always said, when there was trouble, choose the kindest path and the other party will more than likely do the same.

Eva's pinched expression made it clear that kindness was the last thing on her mind.

Bitsie poked her head through the swinging kitchen door. "Rebecca, is everything all right?"

With coffee dripping from my arm and my now-empty cup rolling on the ground, she could see it wasn't, but she wasn't looking at me. She was watching Eva Henriksen.

Eva was glaring back, her expression stuck somewhere between confusion and anger.

Was this on my account? Or was something else going on here?

Even the man at the counter seemed interested in the strange standoff.

For one long, strained moment, no one moved. No one spoke until Bitsie finally waved at me. "Come on back, dear. Let's get some water on that stain before it sets."

"I really am sorry, Ms. Henriksen," I said, though I wasn't sure what I was apologizing for. The coffee had completely missed her, but maybe I had startled her as much as she had startled me. "I hope I didn't hurt you. Are you all right?"

That tiny woman turned her glare from Bitsie to me, her nostrils flared, and she stiffened to her full five-feet-nothing height.

"I'm fine, no thanks to you." Then she spun around and marched down the street without looking back.

It was as close to a verbal slap in the face as I'd ever had. I walked back to Bitsie in a daze. I didn't know what to say to her, except to apologize. Apparently, that was all I was capable of doing. "I'm so sorry for the trouble."

"Don't worry about a thing, dear. You just set your things here." She tapped the counter behind the register. "Accidents happen. That woman just…" Her lips clamped together, and she shook her head. Instead of finishing her sentence, she led me back into the kitchen.

It was smaller than I'd imagined. Only about half the space of the dining room and crammed full of stainless-steel counters and shelves, along with the biggest stove I'd ever seen in my life. Hank and Luna were at the back, standing near boxes of glass jars filled with a dark red sauce, all featuring labels that resembled the diner's logo. They were so engrossed in their own conversation, they didn't seem to notice Bitsie or me.

"Do you know Ms. Henriksen?" I asked Bitsie as we passed the other two and slipped into an adjoining room with an industrial-size sink and chrome shelves filled with plates, glasses, and stacks of towels and napkins.

"She used to come in with Gunther," Bitsie replied. "And she would give Hank and his staff such a difficult time. Always complaining about something. I don't know about you, but I find it's best to steer clear of people like that. Too much trouble." She grabbed a clean, white towel from the edge of the sink, soaked it under the faucet, and dabbed at the coffee spots on my sleeve.

"I just met her yesterday." Did being questioned by the police at the same time in a dead man's house count as meeting someone? Apparently, it was enough for that someone to spread lies about me to the police.

I should have asked her why she'd done it. It would have been the perfect opportunity, but I'd been too flustered. Some Adelaide Morris I was turning out to be.

"Are you sure you're all right? You're looking rather pale." Bitsie reached up and smoothed a chunk of hair that had fallen over my cheek and swept it back behind my ear. It was the sort of thing my mother would have done.

"I'm fine. Just embarrassed, I guess." I glanced back at the door and saw the man who had been reading the newspaper had found a mop and was cleaning the puddle of coffee. He had also donned a red apron, like the one Hank wore.

"Like I said, these things happen to everybody. Don't give it another thought. And the good news is, I can't even see the stain. Can you?"

The lower part of my sleeve was soaking wet, but I couldn't see the stain, either. "You got it out. Thank you."

"Glad to help." She twisted the excess water out of the towel. "They keep the dirty laundry in the other room. I'll be back in a minute. Could you grab one of the clean towels from the shelf and leave it on the sink?"

As she walked out, I went to the chrome shelves to get the towel. One shelf had folded aprons, packages of napkins, and trays of utensils. Another plates and cups. I didn't see any towels.

Ducking down to check the lower shelf, I found jugs of cleaning liquid and dish soap and, surprisingly, a carton of imported tomatoes in jars. Wedged in the corner beside them was a plain cardboard box. I peeked inside and saw stacks of label rolls.

I pulled one out for a look. It was the label I'd seen on the spaghetti sauce jars. It resembled the diner's logo, but in the center, instead of the front end of a classic car, it featured an older woman with a 1940s hair roll. MAMA MALONE'S MARINARA arched over the top of the image. In smaller letters beneath it, it read, A FAMILY RECIPE FROM THE OLD

Country.

I was no marketing expert, but I could picture that woman standing over a huge pot of sauce, stirring with a long wooden spoon. I'd definitely trust her with my pasta. Whatever Hank was charging for those jars, it probably wasn't enough.

When I went to put the labels back in the box, I lost my balance and grabbed the shelf's edge to steady myself. I didn't fall, but I managed to knock over a few jars of tomatoes. I put them back, but as I pulled the last from where it was leaning into a half-open cardboard box lodged behind the box of labels, I noticed that smaller box was covered in something slimy. And fuzzy?

What was that?

Carefully, I pulled the smaller box out to have a look. Inside was an opened jar of tomatoes, or at least I think it was tomatoes. All I could see now was fuzzy, mucky mold.

I'd never seen so much mold.

My first instinct was to pull it out and throw it away, then tell Hank about it. Surely, he'd want to know what was lurking at the back of his shelves.

But then I second-guessed myself.

I'd just made a scene and a mess in his restaurant, and now I was going to make another scene? These people didn't know me, not really, and the last thing I wanted was to become known as a troublemaker like Eva Henriksen. I also didn't want to embarrass Hank in front of Bitsie or Luna.

Especially Luna.

No, I didn't have to be the one to give him this unfortunate news. But I could pull it to the front of the shelf and make it more visible, so the next time he—or anyone—checked these shelves, they'd find it themselves.

"Is everything all right, Rebecca?" Bitsie reentered the room.

"Everything's fine." I finished moving the boxes and spotted the clean towels on the top shelf. I pulled one down and draped it over the sink's rim.

"Are those the labels?" Bitsie was looking at a roll I'd set on a shelf. I must have put it there when I lost my balance. "They're absolutely darling." She grabbed the roll and left the room.

I followed Bitsie to the kitchen, where she had interrupted Luna and Hank's conversation. "You created these? On your own?"

Luna blushed. "Hank helped. He knew what he wanted and had a great picture of his mother. I just followed his directions."

He shook his head. "No way. It was all her. She took what I had and made it look amazing."

"Well, they're marvelous," Bitsie said. "Don't you agree, Rebecca?"

"Makes me want to buy one."

"See?" Bitsie said to Hank. "What did I tell you? These jars are going to be a hit. Your mother would be so pleased to know you've brought her recipe back. I'm sure it makes your dad happy too."

"On his good days." He glanced up at the wall clock. "Which reminds me, I need to get back before his nurse leaves for the day. If you'll excuse me." He pulled off his apron as he headed for the door. When he passed Luna, he swept up her hand and planted a kiss on her knuckles. "Thanks for stopping by. Can I call you later?"

"Of course," she said sweetly. "Go take care of your dad."

"I will. Bye, Ms. Baynor, Rebecca." He tapped the shoulder of the man who had finished cleaning up my spill and was now in the midst of making a new pot of coffee. "The kitchen's all yours, Gil."

Gil gave his boss a casual salute as Hank made his way to the back door.

When Hank was gone and Gil went back to work, the rest of us looked at each other.

"I should be getting back, too," I said, inching toward the front door. "Thank you for your help, Ms. Baynor. And it was nice to meet you, Luna."

Bitsie followed me. "What's the rush, dear? We're all going to the same place, aren't we? Let's walk together. After all, we're practically family now."

CHAPTER THIRTEEN
Stranger Danger

STIRLING MET ME at the door when I returned to the shop. "Good. You're back," he said with a stern look in his eyes.

Uh-oh. Had he discovered my stray kitten? During the walk back from Malone's with Bitsie and Luna, I'd realized how foolish it was to try to keep her a secret. I should have just told him and been done with it instead of playing games. Maybe it wasn't too late. "Stirling, there's something—"

He raised his hand to stop me, and that's when I realized he was carrying his hat and tweed coat. "I'm sorry to do this to you, but could you watch the store for me? Just for a bit. Thank you, Rebecca. I don't know what I'd do without you."

"You're leaving?" He brushed past me with little more than a glance. He didn't ask about the Malone's takeout bag or what had happened at the police station. "Are you going to the apartment?"

"No, no. I'm feeling fine. It's just an errand that can't

wait," he said on his way out. "Nothing to be concerned about."

He thought I was worried about his health, and I was, but I was also worried he'd find Aneksi, if he hadn't already. I'd left her sleeping in his guest bathroom.

I hadn't intended to leave her alone for so long. I had planned to talk with him first thing this morning and ask his permission to bring her into the store, where I could keep an eye on her. She seemed to have recovered from last night's ordeal, but if she took a turn for the worse, I wanted to take her to a vet.

That was all before my surprise visit from Detective Devon, however. "When will you be back?" Could he hear the desperation in my voice?

He waved goodbye but didn't answer. He didn't even slow down.

I watched him dart along the sidewalk and disappear around the corner. Wherever he was going, he was in a hurry to get there, which meant my sweet little guest would have to stay in that bathroom a bit longer. I really hoped she was all right.

As I stood in the doorway, holding the food from Malone's and wondering where my grandfather was going, Bitsie stepped out of her shop with a water bowl that she set near her door.

"Was that Stirling I saw leaving? Do you know when he'll be back?" For the first time, she sounded unsure of herself. She fidgeted with a fake red hibiscus she'd tucked behind her ear since our walk.

"That was him, but he didn't say when he'd be back."

"What a shame. I wanted to invite him over for tea since it seems we're in for another slow afternoon. I found a Mexican orange blossom tisane in Ensenada last week. I thought he might enjoy it." She placed a water bowl beneath her glass window.

Tisane? I guess that had something to do with tea. "That's very nice of you. I'll let him know when he gets back, whenever that is. Is that for your dog?"

She gave me a funny look, so I pointed at the bowl.

"Oh, no. It's for the dogs out on their walks with their people, and cats, too. We have some strays in the area, and I worry about them, being out in the elements all alone. You might have noticed some of them."

Only the one currently stashed in Stirling's apartment. "No, but I'll keep my eye out. Maybe I can get Stirling to put out a water bowl, too. That's a really kind thing to do."

"Yes, you should do that. I'm sure our furry friends would appreciate it. Maybe I'll pop over a little later to see if Stirling's back." There was that enigmatic grin again. Did she not trust me to deliver the message? Or was I being overly sensitive?

Either way, I wondered if Stirling realized he had an admirer. Men could be so oblivious about that kind of thing. I'd had to walk by Mason's high school football practice for a month before he noticed me.

If only I could go back and tell my sophomore self he wasn't worth the trouble.

I tried to ignore the sting of that old memory as I closed the door, stuffed our food into the miniature fridge in the office, gave the outside of my purse a thorough cleaning with every spray and powder we had in the storage room, and then did my best to wait patiently for Stirling to get back.

It wasn't easy.

All he expected me to do was ring up sales, but since the shop was empty and I had nothing to keep me company but my thoughts, I kept myself busy the only way I knew how.

First, I took a dusting cloth to the set of stone canopic jars. Then I ran the sweeper over the shop floor. I even wiped down the cash register while I waited.

When the door chime rang about an hour later, I popped up from behind the display of ceramic scarabs I was rearranging, but it wasn't Stirling. It was a statuesque woman looking for a gift for her husband to help announce a trip to Japan she'd purchased for their twentieth wedding anniversary. After considering a few items I suggested, she left with a hundred-year-old jade dragon. One of the finest pieces in Stirling's Asian collection, and also one of the priciest.

I was still feeling proud of myself an hour later when a man in a linen suit entered and lingered in the Egyptian section.

"Is this new?" he asked as he examined a five-foot-tall

statue of Anubis positioned beside the cash register.

"It depends on what you mean by new. It was made during the Egyptian Revival period, which would date it to the late nineteenth century or early twentieth century."

All those hours spent lurking among the history books in my parents' store were paying off. I couldn't resist sharing a little more.

"The Egyptian aesthetic was very popular during that period. I'm sorry I can't be more specific. I could check with my grandfather when he returns and get back to you."

His lips disappeared beneath his dark, bushy mustache. "I meant, is it new to the shop? I haven't seen it here before."

So much for my pride.

He started to walk away then turned back. "Did you say Stirling Cuthbert is your grandfather? I wasn't aware he had family nearby."

"We only connected recently."

His lips reappeared in a slow, creeping smile. "How delightful. Life can be so full of surprises. Are you expecting him back soon?"

"I am." Prickles inched up the back of my neck. This man seemed more interested in Stirling than the Anubis. "You're welcome to wait, but I really can't say how long it might be."

He checked his watch, a sleek black and gold timepiece that looked like it was worth more than my car. "I'm afraid I won't have time for that."

That was a relief. "If you'd like to leave a message, I'll be sure he gets it."

There was nothing overtly threatening about him, but the guy gave me the creeps. I moved back behind the counter, where Stirling kept a can of pepper spray for emergencies. I'd never used one before, but I was sure I could figure it out if the need arose.

He watched me intently, as if he were reading my thoughts. "That won't be necessary. I'll stop by another time. Thank you, Rebecca. You've been very helpful." He tipped the brim of his straw Panama hat and left.

As I watched him walk away, I wasn't sure how I'd been helpful, but I definitely knew I had not told that man my name.

CHAPTER FOURTEEN
Neighborly Offer

S TIRLING STILL HADN'T returned when it was time to close the shop, so I ran the end-of-day report from the cash register and pulled in the standing sign from the sidewalk.

While I was outside, Bitsie walked out with a water pitcher to refill the water bowl near her door. The hibiscus was missing from her ear. "Still no sign of your grandfather?"

She was persistent, I'd give her that. "Not yet. I wasn't expecting him to be gone this long. Any idea where he might have gone?"

She finished filling the bowl. "Me? Goodness, no. But it's not like him. He rarely leaves the shop. I hope everything is all right. You look worried."

Hiding my emotions had never been one of my strengths. "I guess I am," I confessed. But my concern for my grandfather was only one of an ever-growing list of worries. Aneksi, the police, my crumbling life. It made me dizzy if I thought about it too long.

"Are you hungry?" she asked.

"Excuse me?"

"Have you eaten anything since this morning? My guess is you haven't. What do you say to a scoop or two of ice cream?"

The churning in my stomach reminded me the woman was right. I'd eaten one of the orders of custard French toast, which was as delicious as Officer Meadows promised, and considered digging into the one I'd brought for Stirling, but I couldn't bring myself to open the refrigerator door. Seeing the box of tuna for Aneksi made me feel so guilty, I'd powered through the day without lunch, figuring if she was hungry, joining her involuntary fast was the least I could do.

As tempting as Bitsie's offer was, I had to get back to Aneksi. "I would love to, but I can't. There's something I need to do back at Stirling's place."

Bitsie waved off my refusal. "There's no hurry. Go take care of whatever it is you need to do then come back. We're checking inventory, so I'll be around for a while."

"Are you sure?" Inventory at the bookstore was always a lengthy and agonizing process.

"Absolutely. When you come back, just knock. I'll be here."

"Thank you. That's very kind."

"Not really. You'll be doing me a favor. Inventory is my very least favorite job, and I could use the distraction."

"Well, if you're sure. It won't take me long."

"Good. I'll look forward to it." She offered a hint of a smile. "You know, we were voted best ice cream in town by the Citrus Grove Gazette." She pointed to the quote painted on her glass window.

It was an odd claim to fame for a memorabilia store, but what did I know?

Once I finished closing up Cuthbert Exotic Antiques, I hurried to Stirling's apartment and found Aneksi curled on the blanket, exactly where I'd left her. When I spoke her name, she didn't move. My heart flipped a somersault.

I dropped down beside her. "Aneksi," I whispered again. Sure, it was an imaginary name invented by a hallucination, but it was better than no name at all.

When she still didn't stir, I touched her back, hoping to feel the rise and fall of her breath. Then one furry ear perked.

She was alive.

Relieved, I darted to the kitchen to transfer the tuna in the Malone's box to a plate. When I returned, I nudged the fish toward her nose. At first, she only stretched and butted the top of her head against my fingers, coaxing them to scratch her. Once I obliged, her eyes fluttered open.

"I brought you some food," I whispered.

She stretched again, then rose and nibbled at the fish.

I hadn't expected her to answer, but I still breathed easier when she didn't. At least I was past whatever nonsense had caused those hallucinations.

While she ate, I stroked her back. Her fur was clean and

even fluffier than it had been, and now that she was up, she seemed to be recovered from whatever had ailed her when she crawled into the back of my car.

Just to be sure, I pulled her away from the plate and sat her on my lap. I gazed into her bright blue eyes. "Are you really better?"

She sat on my thighs and kneaded my blue jeans with her front paws. Then that purr motor revved up.

"You know I can't keep you, right? This is only temporary." I don't know if I was saying that for her benefit or my own. The plan was to keep her overnight and get her to a vet, but now that a vet didn't seem necessary, I didn't know what I was going to do.

I knew what I *wanted* to do, but I wasn't prepared to take care of a cat. I wasn't even prepared to take care of myself. Responsible pet owners weren't the kind of people who packed a bag and ran away from their problems on a moment's notice.

Aneksi needed a good home with someone who didn't leave her alone all day and who didn't have to buy her dinner at a diner. She deserved someone better than me.

But unless I figured out a way to prove Eva Henriksen was lying about me to the police, I wasn't going to be around long enough to find her a proper home. I'd be in jail.

So, that had to take priority right now. Luckily for me, Bitsie Baynor might be able to help. If I told her my predicament, maybe she could help me figure out how to prove I didn't deliver Stirling's stolen statue to Gunther. Maybe then the detective would realize Eva Henriksen had probably implicated me to cover for somebody else. It was the only explanation that made sense.

Since Bitsie obviously knew the woman, I was hoping she might know who Eva was protecting.

I lifted Aneksi gently from my lap, and she stirred from her slumber.

"You have food now, but I still have to keep you in here. Just for a little while longer. Will you be all right?"

That soft, furry head lifted, and she rubbed her cheek against the side of my hand. I took it as a yes.

CHAPTER FIFTEEN

Ice Cream Confessions

T HE MEMORABILIA SHOP'S door was locked when I returned, but the lights were on. When I knocked, Luna popped up from behind a glass case of Elvis cookie jars and salt and pepper shakers.

She came to the door with a clipboard in one hand and a pen in the other and let me in.

"Bitsie asked me to stop by," I said. "Is she still here?"

"She's here somewhere," Luna said and looked back over her shoulder, past the Elvis souvenirs and the life-sized cardboard cutouts of the Three Stooges, Humphrey Bogart, and Bing Crosby.

I'd walked by the Golden Oldies Memorabilia Shoppe dozens of times, but this was the first time I'd been inside. It had seemed smaller from the outside, but now I could see it was only because every square inch of the place was packed with merchandise, including the walls, which were covered in old movie posters and autographed black and white images of celebrities like Doris Day, Rock Hudson, and

Raquel Welch in their heyday.

As Luna led me deeper into the store, toward the back rooms, I admired the bobble head Beatles, a James Dean lamp, and a Lucille Ball tea set.

When I stopped to marvel at the standing Elvis clock, with its rocking pelvis pendulum, I lost sight of Luna.

"Back here," she hollered and waved her hand over her head.

I found her near the back, past an old-fashioned ice cream cart with three bistro tables set around it.

I followed her to the corridor, which was covered in blue plastic tarps with a can of paint pushed against the wall. A redecorating project seemed to be underway.

Luna opened the first door on the right and poked her head into the room. "There you are, Bitsie. Rebecca from next door is here to see you."

"Already? Tell her I'll be out in a moment."

"Oh, well, she's right here." Luna leaned back so I could wave at Bitsie, who was in an apron and standing at a wall with a chisel in her hand. Her eyes went wide at the sight of me, then glanced back at the wiring, pipes, and ducts you could see through gashes in the damaged drywall.

"I hope I didn't catch you at a bad time," I said.

If she was worried about hiding the mess from me, she didn't need to be. My dad was always fixing something at our old house. I was no stranger to renovation projects.

Then I heard another voice coming from inside.

I was mortified. "I'm so sorry," I rushed to say. "I didn't mean to interrupt you."

"No, no. You aren't interrupting." She nudged a box against the wall then pulled off her apron, brushed away the drywall dust from her sleeves, and plumped her platinum curls. "I was just clearing away some of the old plaster."

"But if you have another visitor—" I added until she shook her head.

"No visitors. Just me." She pulled the door all the way, revealing the empty room.

There was no doubt about it. She was definitely alone.

"Are you all right?" she asked me.

Was I? I had hallucinated a talking cat and now I was hearing voices. I tried to laugh. "Sure, of course. Why wouldn't I be?" That sounded less confident than I'd hoped.

She gave me a quizzical look. "Actually, you have caught me a bit off guard. This"—she held out her hands, indicating the room—"I was hoping to make it a surprise for Stirling. I don't think he realizes this room is here. We certainly didn't, not until we removed some old wallpaper along that wall and discovered the door to this darling little space. I think it will make a wonderful storage area or second office, once we fix it up."

I shook my head, confused. "And this is for Stirling? I don't understand."

"It's not for him, per se," she said. "But since he's the landlord, I'm sure he'll be delighted to hear we've discovered this new space."

"Wait. He's your landlord?"

"Of course! He owns the whole building."

It made sense that he would own the space that housed Cuthbert Exotic Antiques. The shop had been in his family—our family—for at least two generations before him. But the whole building?

"Would you do me the teensiest of favors, though?" Bitsie was exiting the room now and pulling the door closed behind her. "Please don't say anything until the work is done. I don't want him to see it like this. I want to have it all finished and looking spiffy."

"Sure, I won't say anything. It's very nice of you to fix it up. Most tenants wouldn't go to the trouble."

"Well, he's been a very good landlord, and who knows? Maybe one day he'll be a very good friend, as well."

The twinkle in her eye suggested she meant more than friends.

"Have you had any luck finding someone who can hang the cabinets?" Luna peered around Bitsie to get a look at the ragged walls before the door closed.

"Almost. I've finally found one who says he has experience with the city's rules on historic preservation. That's been the tricky thing about this project. The city requires repairs to preserve the original design of these old buildings."

"I hope this one works out," Luna said, sounding less than confident. "If he doesn't, maybe it wouldn't hurt to have Rebecca ask her grandfather to recommend someone. He must have contacts."

"Absolutely not," Bitsie said. "I'm capable of finding a contractor on my own."

"But it's been two months," Luna said, then stopped. "You're right. I'm sure you'll find someone."

"Besides, there's no rush. We've made do without the space until now. We can wait a little longer." Bitsie hoisted a box sitting near the doorway.

Luna stared in horror. "That's so heavy, Bitsie. Let me help you."

The older woman swiveled away from Luna's reach. "Don't be ridiculous. I'm not an old lady, so please don't treat me like one."

Luna backed off. "I never said you were old."

"Of course not," Bitsie agreed. "Why would you? My doctor says I have the mind and body of a thirty-five-year-old."

I stared at the ground so my expression wouldn't give my thoughts away. Thirty-five? Really? I doubted it, but I wasn't going to say so.

As we passed a rack of Elvis aprons, ceramic trivets, and coffee mugs, Luna said, "Age is only a number. What's in that box, anyway? I thought we were taking inventory not adding to it."

"It's just a few things I picked up on my trip. I came across an incredible flea market in Ensenada. The vendor gave me a great price on these."

Bitsie set the box on a bistro table and opened it. Luna peered over her shoulder and winced. "More black velvet Elvis paintings?"

Luna sounded less than enthusiastic—much less—and I could see why. More than half the wall behind the main Elvis display was already covered in black-velvet artwork.

"What can I say?" Bitsie said. "They're classic kitsch, and kitsch never goes out of style, especially when it features the King. Besides, I think Mayor Wooster will have a special interest in these. The quality is exceptional."

They looked pretty similar to other black-velvet portraits to me, but I certainly wasn't a black-velvet art expert.

Considering the overwhelming amount of merchandise she had that was dedicated to Elvis, I figured she had to know what she was talking about.

Bitsie slanted Luna a coy smile. "Have I ever told you I was in a movie with Elvis?"

"You might have mentioned it," Luna said in a way that made me think her boss had definitely mentioned it and probably more than once.

"It was *Speedway*, one of my first acting jobs when I came to Hollywood. Elvis was already a big deal, and, boy, did he know it. He was such a flirt. Of course, I was a knockout back then. Blond and almost eighteen. No one knew that, though, because I lied about my age. Everybody did back then. He was married, so I didn't let it go anywhere, but it sure helped me get the director's attention. I had my pick of roles after that. Oh, to be that young again."

Luna pointed to a framed photograph along the wall of a glamorous young blond in a pink cashmere sweater, black tights, and dance shoes mugging playfully for the camera. "That's Bitsie in *The Blonde Next Door*."

Bitsie beamed. "That should have been my breakout film. A great cast, a stellar crew. The studio spared no expense. I had the best wardrobe people, voice coaches, makeup people, hair people, you name it. Unfortunately, the muckety-mucks at the studio insisted on releasing the same weekend as *Butch Cassidy and the Sundance Kid*. We didn't stand a chance, not that I ever held it against Paul or Robert, of course. They were complete gentlemen."

"You knew Paul Newman and Robert Redford?" I'd never met anyone in the movie business before, let alone someone who was on a first name basis with Hollywood royalty.

"Sure, but Hollywood was so much smaller then. Oh, listen to me. You're not here to listen to me prattle on about the good old days. I believe I promised you ice cream."

"I like the stories. It sounds so glamorous."

"Oh, it was," she said as she brushed the box's dust off her arms.

"I'll unpack," Luna said. "You two go get your ice cream."

"Thank you, dear," Bitsie said and led me over to the ice

PAW, CLAWS, AND CURSES

cream cart as Luna lugged the box to one of the Elvis aisles. Bitsie pulled out a bistro chair for me.

"I didn't even notice you sold ice cream until today," I confessed as I took the seat.

"It's the best marketing investment I ever made," Bitsie said. "Summer is our busiest season, and on those hot days, I put an ice cream sign out front, and the shoppers stream in." She patted the top of the cart. "Once they sit down and soak in all this yesteryear goodness, they can't help but leave with a little something. Now, what's your pleasure?"

The handwritten, chalk menu featured six options. Chocolate, strawberry, vanilla, salted caramel, lemon basil, and pomegranate with dark chocolate chunks.

The last one sounded too good to pass up.

Bitsie nodded with approval. "Ah! You have an adventurous spirit. I knew I liked you for a reason. We always stock the standard three, but for the others, I like to keep things interesting. I haven't tried the pomegranate yet, but it sounds so deliciously decadent, doesn't it? Bowl or sugar cone?"

"Bowl, please." As much as I loved sugar cones, I could never eat the ice cream fast enough. I always ended up with a mess all over my fingers.

She scooped a mound into a pink cardboard bowl and handed it to me with a tiny wooden spoon. "How about you, Luna? Can I tempt you?"

The younger woman was still in the Elvis section, unloading the box of black-velvet paintings. "Not today. I need to get going. I have a class at six."

"Suit yourself." Bitsie looked at me. "Luna's getting her business degree at Richland University."

I glanced at the clock. "But it's already half-past five. Won't you be late?"

"Nah," Luna said. "The campus is only a couple blocks away, and parking is easy this time of day."

"The new merchandise can wait till tomorrow, Luna," Bitsie admonished. "Go."

Luna waved her off, and Bitsie rolled her eyes. She scooped herself a portion of the pomegranate ice cream and grabbed a spoon.

When I saw the meager amount in her bowl, my heart sank. "You didn't have to give me so much. You're too generous."

"Nonsense. You're still young. Enjoy it while you can. Believe me, when you're older, you'll wish you had."

"Oh, Bitsie," Luna chided lightly as she carried the emptied box to the back rooms. "You're going to outlive us all."

Bitsie looked like she was about to say something, then shook her head. "Good luck in class, dear. Thank you for all your help today."

"I'll see you tomorrow." Luna waved at both of us then disappeared into the back.

Bitsie turned back to me. "Now, you've heard all about me. Tell me about you. What brought you to Citrus Grove?"

I poked at the ice cream as I savored the bite still melting on my tongue. It was every bit as good as I'd hoped it would be. "I came to help Stirling," I said before taking another bite. "Other than that, there isn't much to tell." There was no reason to dump my dirty laundry on her. I took another bite and tried to use the extra moments to think of a way to guide the topic to what I really wanted to discuss. "I have to admit, I'm still upset about what happened with Ms. Henriksen today. I don't understand why she dislikes me. I don't even know the woman."

Bitsie nodded as though she understood, but her expression gave little else away.

So, we sat in silence, nibbling our ice cream. Inside, I was begging her to tell me something about that woman, anything that might explain her vendetta against me. But Bitsie said nothing.

When the silence became unbearable, I blurted, "Do you think she might know something about her boss's death?" I could almost see Adelaide Morris shake her head with disappointment, but what else could I do? My efforts at being subtle weren't working.

Bitsie's head popped up. "What makes you think she knows something?"

"Because she lied to the police about me. That's why they called me in. I'm a suspect." The confession rolled out of me like a freight train, and it left me feeling dizzy and a little nauseated. Saying it all aloud made it real. And now that I'd started, I couldn't stop. "I was only at that man's house because he called and said he had something that was stolen from Stirling's shop. He wanted to return it. When I went to get it, I found him. But she told the cops I was the one who gave him that stolen item. They think I stole it. Me." I could hear the hysteria in my voice, but I couldn't help it. I swallowed and tried to compose myself. "She's trying to frame me, and there's only one reason I can think of for her to do that. She must be trying to protect someone. Maybe she's trying to protect herself."

Bitsie's expression told me nothing as I watched her digest my accusation. It was maddening, but I had to stop talking. I'd already said too much, and if I didn't shut up, I'd never learn anything. I did my best to stay quiet.

Bitsie set her ice cream down and folded her hands on the table in front of herself. "What a horrible ordeal. I had no idea you were dealing with all of that."

Was that it? Commiseration was all I was going to get? I forced myself to remain silent. She must have more to say.

Then she sighed. "Who in their right mind would think a darling girl like you could do something as awful as that?"

"But she's convinced them. I need to prove to them that she's lying. It's the only way." I couldn't help myself. If she had any useful information and any inclination at all to help, this was the moment. I held her gaze, silently pleading with her.

She closed her eyes and turned away.

I'd pushed too hard. I'd had an opportunity, and I'd blown it. "I'm sorry," I rushed to say. "I don't know what came over me. I've just been so—"

"No, no," she said softly. "Don't apologize. You've done nothing wrong. Actually..." She stopped and touched her mouth. "I don't think Eva killed Gunther Vernon, but I may know a way for you to find out who did."

CHAPTER SIXTEEN

Frantic Call

THE ICE CREAM did a somersault in my stomach. "You know how to find Gunther's killer?"

Bitsie froze, then touched her forehead and whispered, "Oh dear. Perhaps I shouldn't have said anything. I told myself I wouldn't and look at me. This might destroy Luna if she finds out. She doesn't deserve that. He's already hurt her so much."

He? Who was he? "What do you mean? Someone hurt Luna? When?"

"Not in a physical way. At least not that I know of. But he broke her heart. I don't think he even realizes it, but that's not the point. The damage is done."

"Are you talking about Hank Malone?" Luna had consoled him so tenderly at the restaurant. They were obviously close.

"No, no. Not Hank. Martin."

"Martin Fincher?"

Slowly, she nodded.

Martin Fincher was Stirling's thieving ex-manager. He'd been the one who stole Cleopatra's cat, so it wasn't a total surprise that he knew Gunther Vernon. Bitsie had also mentioned that Martin recommended Luna for the job at her shop. "Are you saying you think Martin killed Gunther?"

Bitsie closed her eyes and remained quiet for an agonizingly long moment. When she looked at me again, she was struggling to smile. "No, but I think he might know something that could help you. You see, Martin and I would chat sometimes when he came in for ice cream, like you and I are now. He always seemed like such a nice young man. I even told Luna she should give him another chance. Men can be so foolish at that age, and he seemed keen to win her back."

"They were romantically involved?" She'd already hinted as much, but I wanted to be sure. "How long ago?"

"A year, perhaps more. But they've known each other for years. Since high school, I think. All of them. Luna, Martin, and Hank, too. I think that's one of the reasons Martin wanted me to hire Luna. He was hoping to rekindle her affections."

"When did she start working for you?"

Bitsie touched her temple. "I hired her in January. So, let's see. That makes it just over three months now. Why?"

"It might be important." Adelaide Morris usually thought so, anyway. She often asked about what the suspects were doing and when they were doing it during her investigations. "Is it possible Luna helped Martin with his…"

"The theft? Absolutely not." She shook her head for emphasis. "I'm sure Luna was completely in the dark."

"Doesn't it seem odd that Martin wanted you to hire her when he did? He must have been planning the theft already."

She sank back in her chair. "Yes, I see what you mean. It is odd timing. But you should know Luna wasn't interested in rekindling anything with him. I don't know all the details, but I got the impression she was troubled by something. I thought it was just her focus on pursuing her education. He, on the other hand, had completely given up on his. He had worked on an archeology degree for a couple years at Richland, but then abandoned it. I overheard them arguing about that a few weeks ago, and that's when I first heard that name, Gunther Vernon."

"Why were they arguing about Gunther?"

She poked her spoon at the ice cream and sighed. "I thought he was a romantic rival, so I asked Martin about it later. That's when he told me Gunther had been one of his professors at Richland. Martin told me he hoped to start his own business with Gunther's help. Luna was trying to talk him out of it, though. That's why they were arguing."

"She didn't want him to leave Stirling's shop?"

"She didn't want him going into business with Gunther. Martin confessed to me that Gunther had been forced to leave the university. He'd been fired during Martin's second year. Something to do with questionable excavation practices during an Egyptian dig. Other faculty members accused him of bringing artifacts into the country illegally."

"Smuggling?" I asked.

She nodded. "Martin lost touch with him after that until Gunther contacted him out of the blue last year. He told Martin he had established a legitimate import business and hoped Martin might steer potential clients his way."

"Gunther wanted Stirling's customers? Did Martin do it?"

"I don't know. And after Martin shared that with me, he was different. He seemed to be afraid of something. He begged me not to mention anything about Gunther to Stirling or to Luna, which seemed odd, especially after..."

Her sentence trailed off, so I finished it for her. "The theft?"

She sighed. "I can't help but wonder if Gunther put Martin up to it. The theft, I mean."

Every one of my investigative instincts was screaming that it was closer to a certainty. "It would explain how Stirling's statue fell into Gunther's hands. But it doesn't explain why he wanted to return it."

Bitsie dropped her spoon into the bowl and pushed the melted, untouched ice cream away. "Maybe they were having second thoughts and wanted to make amends."

"Or maybe it was Gunther who grew a conscience." I mulled that thought over my last bite of ice cream. "Are you sure Martin isn't capable of murder?"

She shook her head sharply. "I have never even seen him

angry. A man with Gunther's past probably has enemies, possibly ruthless enemies. Perhaps one of them showed up at Gunther's house, then attacked and robbed him. If that's what happened, Martin may be hiding out of fear for his own life."

It sounded plausible, especially since the police hadn't been able to find Martin. There was one problem with her scenario, though. "Gunther wasn't robbed. The police said nothing was missing."

"What about Stirling's statue?"

"It was still there. It was destroyed, but it was still there. I saw it myself. The police said it was probably damaged during a struggle."

"Oh, what a shame. Couldn't Stirling fix it? It must be salvageable. Do you have the pieces?"

"The police wouldn't let me take anything. They're part of the crime scene. Maybe we can get them back after the investigation is finished."

"That's ridiculous. The police have no right to do that. Stirling should demand the return of his property."

It was sweet how she rallied to Stirling's defense, but I was pretty sure the police would see it differently.

She stared into the melted pink glob in her bowl then glanced up. Something else was weighing on her. "You'll probably think I'm naive to say this, but my gut tells me Martin is not to blame for this. It was that horrible man's influence. I'm sure of it. Martin has always been such a good boy, and I'd like to help him, if I can. I've tried to reach out to him, but he hasn't returned any of my calls."

"You know how to reach him? Do the police know that?"

She seemed surprised by my reaction. "I don't know. They've never asked me about it."

Of course they didn't. They couldn't even find the police report.

"I think he's hiding because he fears for his life," Bitsie continued. "Luna and I have both tried to reach him, to tell him he should cooperate with the police. We haven't had any luck, but there might still be a way."

"You have to tell the police. They could trace the call." I had no idea if that was true or not, but it seemed like something they should be able to do.

Bitsie shook her head. "I don't think they can, or they would have found him by now."

Considering their track record so far, she was probably right. "What do you suggest?"

She leaned forward and lowered her voice, even though we were alone. "If I could just get him to speak to me, I think I could convince him to turn himself in. He isn't thinking clearly right now because he's probably so afraid. I can only imagine the trouble a man like Gunther Vernon got him into. If Martin tells the police what he knows, I'm sure they'll protect him. That's what witness protection is for, isn't it? I know he'll listen to me if I could just speak to him."

What she said made a lot of sense. If Gunther and Martin were partners, Martin also might know who killed Gunther. "You might be right," I said, "but you said yourself, he's not returning your calls. Stirling said he moved out of his apartment and disconnected his phone."

Bitsie sat silently for a moment, then said, "He disconnected one of his phones."

"Are you saying he has more than one?"

"He called me from a new number after Stirling's incident but before I had learned of it. It was a number I didn't recognize, so I didn't pick up. He left a message, saying goodbye and that he was sorry." She reached down and pulled her cell phone from the pocket of her red cardigan. She tapped the screen and scrolled through her contacts. "I've been trying to call him back, but it always goes to voicemail. I've left messages, as I said, but he's never called back."

"Did you give that number to the police?"

She gripped the phone in both hands. "Not yet. I will, I just want to talk to him first and I was thinking that maybe you can help me do that."

"Me?" Was she crazy? I wasn't going to call the man who robbed my grandfather.

"He doesn't answer when I call, but maybe it's because he recognizes my number. If you call, perhaps he'll pick up."

I thought about it. I didn't want to help the guy who took advantage of my grandfather, but if Bitsie was right and he could identify the real killer, it might be worth a try. At this point, I didn't exactly trust the Citrus Grove police to clear my name for me. Detective Devon seemed far more interested in pinning the whole thing on me. It wasn't the best plan, but it was all I had. I fished my phone out of my purse and dialed the number from her screen.

"Wait." Bitsie's hand shot out, stopping me. "Are you doing it now?"

"Might as well." After four rings, the call went to voicemail. I hung up and redialed. This time, someone answered.

I stared at Bitsie. She stared back.

"May I speak with Mr. Fincher?" I tried to use my most businesslike voice.

Bitsie leaned forward, so close the fumes from her hair spray nearly knocked me out. I pulled back.

"Who is this?" the man demanded.

"My name is Rebecca. I'm calling in reference to Gunther Vernon. I understand he was a professor when Mr. Fincher attended Richland University." I didn't know why the university connection popped into my mind, but I didn't want him to think I was with the police.

"How did you get this number?"

I couldn't tell him it was Bitsie, but I had to say something. My mind raced, then I blurted, "A mutual friend said you might be able to help me."

She sat across from me, watching every move.

"Are you with the police?" he asked. "You have to tell me if you are. It's entrapment if you don't." That panicked tone sounded like a man with a guilty conscience.

"I'm not with the police. I'm a reporter." I winced. It was still a lie, but what else could I say? *I'm the granddaughter of the man you robbed?* That wasn't going to win him over. "I need your help, Mr. Fincher."

"Help with what?"

I swallowed hard. "I'm looking into the murder of Gunther Vernon."

There was silence on the line.

Then, "What's your name again?"

"Rebecca." I didn't dare tell him I was a Cuthbert. Luckily, he didn't ask for a last name.

Bitsie leaned forward, but her expression remained unchanged. How could she be so calm? My heart felt like it was going to thump right out of my chest.

"Why do the police think he was murdered?" Martin asked.

I thought I was the one asking the questions. "There was a witness. Not to the murder itself, but soon after."

"Did they find anything?"

"Like a weapon? I don't think so."

"Anything else?"

What was he getting at? Then it occurred to me. He was trying to ask about the statue. "The woman who found him said he had been expecting her. She said she was there to retrieve something that had been taken from Cuthbert Exotic Antiques. Is that what you mean?" I held my breath, praying he wouldn't hang up.

"You're lying," he said. "Or she's lying. Gunther wouldn't do that."

"She was very clear, Mr. Fincher."

Silence stretched between us. Any second he was going to hang up, and I'd be back at square one.

"Was anyone else at Gunther's house?"

"A house … sorry, a domestic manager named Eva Henriksen. Do you know her?"

"That's it? No one from the university?"

"Was someone from the university supposed to be there?"

"Dr. Omar. Gunther brought him in to authenticate an artifact."

The artifact you stole from my grandfather? The words were on the tip of my tongue, and it took every ounce of self-control to hold them back.

"I told him he was being an idiot," Martin snapped. "Once Omar got a look at what we … I mean, he had, he'd want it for himself. I wouldn't put it past that old geezer to make the attack look like a break-in so he could steal it."

"Are you talking about the Egyptian cat statue? No one took that. It was still there. Broken, but still there."

"Broken?" He sounded as incredulous as Stirling had. "Are you sure?"

I gulped. "The woman mentioned it. She described a statue of a cat made of wood with painted features. Is that the one?"

"That's it. Then it must be loose."

"What's loose?"

He paused for a long moment then said, "Ask Stirling Cuthbert."

My heart nearly stopped. I glanced up at Bitsie. Had she heard that? I couldn't tell. "Why?" I asked.

"He's the one who was hiding it. It's cursed, you know. He's cursed. That whole place is cursed."

"You aren't making sense, Mr. Fincher. What do you mean cursed?"

That caught Bitsie's attention. She stiffened.

"It's a monster," he said. "The thing is a monster. I didn't know until it was too late."

"Martin, slow down. I don't understand what you mean. Who's the monster?"

The guy sounded like he was hyperventilating.

"I have to go," he said. "This is all my fault. It's probably after me. I have to get out of here!"

He was quickly spiraling into hysteria.

"Listen to me," I said as calmly as I could. "Who is the monster?" Was it Dr. Omar? Was it Stirling?

"Don't you know?" he whispered frantically. "You have to help me. If you found me, they can, too. I have to get out of here."

"I'll help you, Martin, but you'd have to tell me where you are."

Bitsie nodded, silently urging me on.

"I need to leave," he repeated, but he seemed lost in his paranoia. "The airport. I'll go to the airport. I'll buy a ticket anywhere and just go."

"I'll take you to the airport," I said. "I'll help you. Tell me where you are."

Bitsie slid forward again.

"Now?" he asked. "No, not now. I have to pack. I have to cover my tracks, so they won't find me."

"All right, tell me where you are and when to be there."

"Don't tell anyone. Do you promise? No one."

"I won't. I promise." I gave Bitsie a helpless look. She looked so panicked. I could only imagine how worried she was. "I won't tell anybody. I'll help you. But you have to tell me what this is about."

"Not over the phone. Pick me up at ten thirty tomorrow morning. I'll explain everything then. Remember, don't tell anyone."

"I know. I understand."

He rattled off an address.

"Wait, I need a pen."

As I fished through my purse, Bitsie darted off and returned quickly with a pen and a pad of paper. I mouthed, *thank you*, as she slid them in front of me.

"Okay, give me the address again." I didn't recognize it,

but I was sure I could find it. My freedom depended on it.

"Don't be late," he warned. "And don't forget your promise."

"I won't," I said. "You can trust me."

CHAPTER SEVENTEEN
Market Mishap

AFTER I HUNG up, the gravity of what I'd done settled over me. Martin Fincher apparently knew something about Gunther Vernon's murder, and if I could find out what it was, it might help me clear my name with the Citrus Grove Police Department.

That was the good news.

The bad news was I had agreed to drive the man who stole valuable artifacts from my grandfather to an airport where he, by his own admission, intended to flee the area, maybe the country. Pretty sure that was going to make me some kind of accessory.

Even Bitsie seemed alarmed. "Perhaps it would be better if I did this," she said gently. "I don't want to put you in an awkward position."

Awkward? That was an understatement. As much as I wanted to backpedal out of my promise, it was the only way to find out what he knew, and if I got him into my car alone, he'd have to talk to me. Besides, he sounded like he was afraid of Gunther's killer, which meant he wasn't the killer. That was something. "I appreciate your concern, but I need to do this." I handed back her pen and ripped the page off the notepad. "It'll be all right."

I kept telling myself that as I thanked her for the ice cream and assured her I would convey the message to him that she wanted to help.

She wanted more than assurances, though. "No matter what he says, you must call me when you're with him," she begged. "Don't let him leave without speaking to me first."

"I promise. I'll call you as we're driving. He'll be a captive audience."

That seemed to pacify her, but she made me repeat the promise again as she walked me to the door. Finally, she seemed satisfied. "Thank you for all you've done, Rebecca." She took my hand as we said our goodbyes. "You're truly a lifesaver."

"I just made the call. It was your idea, and you knew how to reach him. He's lucky to have a friend like you."

She smiled one of those serene, almost stoic smiles. "Still, I couldn't have done it without you. We make a good team."

"We do," I said as she closed the shop door behind me and locked it.

Martin wasn't the only lucky one, I thought as I waved goodbye. Thanks to Bitsie, my prospects with the Citrus Grove Police Department were looking a whole lot better. Maybe I wouldn't have to spend the rest of my life in prison after all.

Before heading back to Stirling's apartment, I peeked through the Cuthbert Exotic Antiques window. The shop was dark, just as I'd left it, which meant Stirling hadn't returned. The apartment windows over the barbershop were also dark, so he probably wasn't there, either.

He'd been gone all day, and I had no idea where. The hardest part was, I didn't even know how concerned I should be. Was this unusual for him? Typical? There was still so much I didn't know about the man.

If I was being honest, I was a tiny bit relieved, considering I still hadn't told him about Aneksi. The prospect of doing that was becoming more and more difficult. What if he told me I had to get rid of her? I couldn't imagine putting her back on the street.

She'd made such an improvement after a single decent meal. Which reminded me. I'd fed her the last of the tuna, so I needed to stop by the market for more.

At least it was within walking distance, so I wouldn't lose my parking space. And it was actually a nice time for a walk. The sun was beginning to set, which cast a warm glow over the fountain and the small park at the center of the traffic circle. As the palm, elm, and eucalyptus trees swayed in the gentle breeze, the streetlights and store signs were flickering to life.

A horn blast startled me from my thoughts and sent me stumbling back onto the curb. Apparently, I'd been so distracted, I'd nearly stepped in front of a driver making a right turn out of the roundabout.

"Miss Cuthbert?"

I whipped around at the sound of my name, and my heart sank at the sight of the last person I wanted to see standing behind me. "Detective Devon. Are you following me?"

He smirked. "Why? Should I?" He looked the same as he had that morning, when he'd all but accused me of Gunther Vernon's murder, except he'd traded his blazer for a dark navy windbreaker.

"Do you harass all your out-of-town visitors, or am I special?" My words sounded harsher than I'd intended, but what did he expect? I was trying to mind my own business.

He rolled his eyes. "I'm not harassing you, Miss Cuthbert. I'm just walking. You seem like you might need a refresher course on traffic rules, though. But then, looking both ways before crossing the street should be common sense."

My cheeks burned.

He rubbed his forehead. "I'm sorry. That was rude."

An apology? That was new.

"It's all right. I deserved it. I wasn't paying attention. But if you'll excuse me, I was on my way to the market." I made a point of checking both directions before I started across the street again.

He came up beside me on the curb. "Mind if I join you?

I need a few things myself."

I wasn't in the mood for company, but how could I refuse without looking like I was hiding something?

It didn't matter because he didn't wait for an answer. He darted across the street during a break between cars then looked back to see why I was still on the curb. "Are you coming?"

Nope, I didn't have a choice. "Yeah, I'm coming."

He didn't say anything when I fell in step beside him, which was fine by me. Actually, I hoped we could walk the whole way in silence. The last thing I wanted to do was let something slip about Martin Fincher.

After a couple minutes, Detective Devon glanced down at me. "We got off on the wrong foot this morning, and I'd like to apologize for that. It's a difficult case, and I was taking it out on you. I shouldn't have."

Another apology? This was getting weird.

"Don't worry about it. I'm the one who forgot our appointment."

He shoved his hands into his front pockets as we passed an antique store with a window full of Victorian and Edwardian furniture.

"So, how are you liking Citrus Grove?"

Oh no. Small talk. I was terrible at small talk. "It's nice. Not what I expected, but nice."

"Really? What were you expecting?"

I winced. I should have stopped at nice. "I thought there

would be more surf, I guess. More sand."

A laugh rumbled through that bodybuilder chest of his. Not that I was staring at his chest, but the way the buttons of his blue button-down shirt seemed to be holding on for dear life made it hard not to notice. "It's not Laguna or Newport Beach, I'll give you that. Are you disappointed?"

"No. I like it." It was the truth. Citrus Grove wasn't what I'd expected. It was actually better. "I didn't know places like this still existed, and the people couldn't be nicer. It's really…" I tried to think of a different word but couldn't. "It's really nice."

"Except for the murders."

"Right. Except for that." I stared at the tips of my white sneakers, hoping he wasn't insinuating that I was the murderer. "Since you brought it up, may I ask how the investigation is going?"

Now it was his turn to stare at his feet. "We're pursuing all possible leads."

That sounded like an official response. "Of course." For a second, I wanted to tell him about Martin.

I wanted him to know there were other suspects he wasn't even considering. But something told me not to do it until I learned more. If all went according to plan, that would be tomorrow morning. I could hold off that long.

The detective and I walked in silence until we reached the brick staircase that led up to the Circle Market's main door, which had been a loading dock back when the place was a warehouse for local citrus growers. It was easy to see that was what it had been because, like many of the historic buildings in the neighborhood, it had preserved some of its original brick and ironwork, as well as what was left of the original Sunkissed Co-op sign.

"Thanks for the company," I said as we passed under the roll-up, metal door. I grabbed a handheld basket from the stack and darted off toward a middle aisle. The whole time, I resisted the urge to look back to see if he was watching me.

But why did I care?

I didn't, I told myself as I navigated to the canned food section to grab more tuna, then found the pet section, where I stocked up on other cat-related supplies. A small bag of kitty litter and a hot-pink litter box, which was, oddly, the only color option. I was halfway to the checkout counter when I spotted a display of candles, bath oils, and lotions. The sign above the display read LET GO AND RELAX.

Mentally, I groused that it was wishful thinking to believe relaxation was as easy as lighting a candle or dribbling scented oil into a bath. Still, I found myself lingering at the display. I lifted one candle after another and sniffed. The one with an earthy, lavender scent was especially nice. Bold letters across its label promised to relieve tension and stress.

Really? I doubted a candle could lift the anvil of tension and stress that had taken up residence on the back of my neck. Still, I dropped the candle into my basket, along with a similarly scented bath bomb, relaxation oil, and hand lotion.

Maybe none of them would work, but I figured they couldn't hurt, either.

As I headed to the checkout counter, I realized I didn't have anything to scoop through the litter. I went back to the pet aisle, and by the time I pulled a spatula-looking thing off the shelf and returned to the register, there was a line. Standing at the end of that line was Detective Devon.

If he hadn't already seen me, I would have spun around and gone back to the pet aisle for a toy or a bed or anything. But he had seen me, and there was a ridiculous grin planted on his face.

Did he know how uncomfortable he made me? It sure seemed like it. Fine. I'd do what my mom always told me to do when my nerves got the better of me. She'd say, "Pretend everything is all right. You might not be able to change how you feel on the inside, but you can change what it looks like on the outside. Sometimes, that's enough."

I hoped it would be enough because that was what I did. I walked up to that smirking detective and planted myself behind him like I didn't have a care in the world.

"May I help you with that?"

I'd been looking the other way, trying to ignore him, so I wasn't even sure he was speaking to me. When I turned, his hazel gaze was directed squarely at me.

"No, I'm good." He might have believed me if the litter box hadn't chosen that moment to topple out of the basket. Then my failed attempt to catch it midair tipped the basket, sending four tuna cans skidding across the polished concrete floor like hockey pucks, with my lavender-scented bounty close behind.

The clatter turned every pair of eyes in the place my direction. Somehow, I chased everything down, and when I returned, Detective Devon handed me the litter box. "Thanks," I muttered without making eye contact.

"Any time."

When the shopper ahead of him had bagged and paid for her items, the detective approached the checkout counter, and I saw what was in his basket. An individual dinner of frozen meatloaf and mashed potatoes and a pint of chocolate milk.

I didn't know they even sold that stuff outside of elementary school cafeterias. If my own ego wasn't so bruised, I might have said something.

The cashier, an older woman with a platinum blond bouffant and bright coral lipstick that matched her perfectly manicured fingernails, gazed at the carton after scanning it. "Chocolate milk? Must be Wednesday."

"You know me so well, Gladys." He winked at her and dropped his items into a reusable shopping bag he'd pulled from his back pocket. When he slung the bag over his arm, he grinned back at me. "Have a good evening, Miss Cuthbert." He gave Gladys a casual salute and headed for the door.

"You're new." She dragged a tuna can across the scanner

and looked at me like I owed her an explanation.

"I am." I dropped my empty basket into a stack at the end of the counter. "I'm just visiting."

"With Stirling Cuthbert?"

Did everybody around here know my grandfather? "How'd you know?"

She grinned, which made her tawny eyes twinkle. "You've got his eyes. As green as the Irish fields. You're lucky you didn't inherit those eyebrows, though." She chuckled.

She wasn't kidding. His eyebrows were thick, wiry things that sat on his forehead like fuzzy caterpillars. "You obviously know my grandfather."

"Sure do. Most people around here know the old-timers, and he's one of the oldest. Didn't know about you, though. But then, Stirling likes to keep his secrets. Do you have a bag?"

I usually paid the extra few cents for the store bags, but there was something in the way she asked that kept me from doing that this time. I pointed to the stand at the end of the counter with reusable grocery bags for sale. "I'll take one of those."

Her lips pulled into that ear-to-ear grin again. "Good choice. Grab whichever one you like."

I picked a sunny yellow one with the town's logo emblazoned across the front and filled it with the smaller items. I tucked the litter box under my arm.

She completed my transaction and handed me the receipt. As I tried to take it, she kept hold of it and met my gaze. "You know, he doesn't often smile like that."

"My grandfather?"

She shook her head. "Nick."

It took me a second to realize Nick was Detective Devon. "Oh." It wasn't the best response, but it was the best I could do, considering I hadn't the faintest idea what she meant.

Finally, she released the receipt. "How long will you be staying, dear?"

I mustered a smile despite the uneasy feeling churning through me. "I'm not sure. Until Stirling gets a new manager, I suppose."

She nodded. "Then we'll be seeing you around, I hope."

"You will. Thanks." I hooked the bag on my arm and left.

"Oh, Rebecca," she called when I was almost through the roll-up door.

Dread crept over me as I turned back.

A shiny coral fingernail pointed to the end of her checkout counter. "You forgot your kitty litter."

CHAPTER EIGHTEEN
Frustrated and Afraid

"SHE WAS DEFINITELY suggesting something," I said as I wedged the litter box into the space between the end of the claw-footed bathtub and the wall in the small bathroom attached to Stirling's guest bedroom.

Aneksi, who I'd found awake and exploring the room when I returned from the market, was sitting primly in the doorway, watching me.

"Why else would she tell me how much he does or doesn't smile?" I reached behind me for the litter bag, tore it open, and poured the dusty gravel into the pink plastic basin. "The guy thinks I'm a murderer, for goodness' sake. He's probably following me, hoping to find evidence to use against me. Or maybe he's just doing it as a public service to be sure I don't kill again. Oh, forget it. Why am I telling you?"

It was the sort of thing I'd tell Lacey. My former best friend was always the voice of reason when I doubted my instincts. Even now, after her betrayal, I missed her.

The cat jumped into the middle of the box and startled me back to the task at hand.

"Yes, this is for you," I said. "Do you like it?"

She pushed at the gravel with hesitation, then gazed up at me. "Perhaps. What is it?"

I nearly fell backward. I'd convinced myself our earlier conversations were figments of my imagination, triggered by exhaustion or stress or both.

But here she was, talking again and sounding shockingly like sweet Miss Marple.

Those blue eyes widened. "Is this supposed to be sand? It does not feel like sand." She stepped on the pebbly surface as if she was walking through something sticky.

"It's a place for you to do your business." Was it a good idea to go along with the hallucination? Probably not, but it was better than sitting here in an empty apartment and worrying about everything that had gone wrong. I'd come to Orange County to get away from my problems, and here I was, surrounded by a whole new batch.

The cat cocked her head to the side. "What is my business?"

My subconscious sure had a mean streak. Fine, two could play that game. I explained what I meant as plainly as possible.

Aneksi lifted her nose. "It is unnecessary. Mistress Cleopatra's handmaidens tend to such things."

Good grief. The Cleopatra thing was getting ridiculous.

"Unfortunately, your mistress isn't here, and neither are her handmaidens. There's only me, so you'll have to get used to using this when nature calls."

She stared at me for a long moment. "Where has she gone?"

"I don't know where she's gone." That was the truth. Technically, nobody knew where Cleopatra had gone. Her final resting place remained a mystery, despite the occasional claims by historians and enthusiasts to the contrary.

"When will she return?"

That question was more difficult to answer. Not because I didn't know, but because of the sadness in that furry creature's voice. It nearly broke my heart. Even if this conversation was all in my head, how could I tell this sweet, little thing that her mistress would never return? That the person she loved most in the world was gone forever?

A wallop of raw emotion caught me by surprise. I tried to force it back with a hard swallow.

Aneksi waited patiently, then dipped her head like a con-spirator. "You like that man, don't you?"

I blinked away something that might have been a tear. "Stirling? Of course I do. He's been wonderful to me."

"Not your grandfather, silly. The detective. You have been thinking of him, yes?"

Where did she get that ridiculous idea? "No! I was just telling you about an interesting conversation I had with the cashier before I came home. That's what people do. They talk about things. All kinds of things. They don't always mean something."

"Sometimes they do."

Was that a smile on her lips? That wicked little minx. Was she trying to make me squirm?

Whatever sympathy I had for her flew out the window. I stood up and rolled the open end of the half-empty litter bag closed. "I don't like him. He thinks I killed a man. How could I like someone who believes I'm capable of that?" I shoved the litter bag into the cabinet beneath the sink, alongside the extra rolls of toilet paper.

She gave me a bored look and strolled back into the bedroom. "If you say so. But it does not look that way to me."

I leaned out the door. "How would you know? You hardly know me."

She jumped onto the bed and licked her paw. "I have seen it on your face when you speak of him."

"Frustration. That's what you're seeing. That's all it is."

She ran her paw over her left ear. "A particular kind of frustration. I have seen it before. He would only cause such emotion if you cared about him. Apparently, you care more than you care to admit."

"Of course I care. He can throw me in jail."

She licked her paw again and ran it over her other ear. "I do not think that is it."

"Think whatever you like. I don't have feelings for Detective Devon, and I don't care what you think."

Even as I said it, I could feel my pulse race and my cheeks burn. I didn't want her to be right, and I certainly didn't want to lose an argument to a hallucination. I felt nothing for that man.

I didn't.

At all.

Okay, he was attractive in a clean-cut, Dudley-Do-Right kind of way. Under different circumstances, I might like him, but there was no way I could ever consider liking a man who wanted to arrest me.

Aneksi had stopped preening to watch me. That penetrating stare gave me the feeling she was eavesdropping on the ridiculous debate going on inside my head.

Was she reading my thoughts?

No, that was crazy. This whole thing was crazy, and if I didn't snap out of it, I was pretty sure I'd go crazy, too.

It was nerves. That was what it was. I was feeling so guilty about keeping Aneksi a secret from Stirling, it was eating me up inside. Add to that the frustrating meeting with Detective Devon and his inept police investigation, all the emotional baggage I brought from Elk Pass, and, worst of all, the growing feeling that meeting Martin Fincher in the morning would be a horrible mistake.

Aneksi was still staring at me, and I could practically see the smirk beneath her whiskers.

"Don't look at me like that," I said. "I have to meet him. He knew Gunther, and he might know who the real killer is.

Okay, yes, there is a possibility that he's the killer, but I don't think so. He's afraid the killer is after him, and he's Bitsie's friend. She doesn't think he's the killer. But why am I trying to convince you? Forget it, I'm going to take a bath."

I grabbed my pajamas and the bag containing all my lavender-scented goodies and locked myself in the bathroom.

When I emerged an hour later after a thorough soaking, my muscles feeling like jelly and my skin smelling like lavender fields, Aneksi was sitting in the same spot with the same expression. Again, I reminded myself our conversations were only hallucinations. None of them were real. She was an ordinary cat, and I was a crazy person.

I slipped on my comfortable jammies and a pair of fuzzy socks before tucking my dirty clothes into the bag I was using as a hamper. Then I settled into bed for a good night's sleep, ready to put the craziness behind me. I turned on the television for some distraction.

Aneksi was still looking at me, and I couldn't shake the feeling that there was judgment in those blue eyes of hers.

I turned to her squarely. "You think I'm making a mistake, don't you?"

This time, I expected her to answer. I expected something.

She said nothing and kept staring.

"I know it's not ideal. I know I shouldn't be meeting Martin, especially behind Stirling's back, but if I don't do this, I'm probably going to prison because the police aren't doing their job. The guy is planning to skip town. If I don't talk to him before he goes, I won't have another chance."

Would she answer? Was I that far gone?

Aneksi only lifted a paw and licked it.

What did I expect? A cat—talking or not—was not going to clear my guilty conscience. What I needed was a good night's sleep. Things would look better in the morning.

I switched off the light and crawled beneath the covers, being careful not to encroach on her space. "Good night, Aneksi."

As my eyes closed and slumber tugged at me, I heard, faintly, "Good night, human."

CHAPTER NINETEEN
Office Visit

SLEEP DID NOT bring the relief I'd hoped it would. In the dark, early morning hours, I'd awakened in a cold sweat and deeply regretted my decision to take Martin to the airport. Even if he knew who Gunther's killer might be, why would he tell me? And there was still the very real possibility that he was the killer.

Yesterday, I'd refused to believe that. He didn't sound like a killer, and Bitsie was convinced he was innocent. But the thought that plagued me all night was that Stirling probably would have said the same thing before Martin betrayed him. As much as I wanted to believe this guy was harmless, he obviously had a dark side.

He had seemed genuinely afraid, however. He'd also seemed particularly afraid of Stirling, which raised even more questions. Had my grandfather been completely honest with me?

As I lay in bed wrestling with my thoughts, they quickly exploded into full-blown fears. One thought I returned to again and again was what might have happened if I'd arrived earlier to Gunther Vernon's house. Would I have walked in on the killer? And if so, would I have been murdered, too?

By sunrise, I'd had enough. I rolled out of bed, ready to put the nightmares behind me, and found Aneksi curled up on the blanket I'd folded on the floor beside me.

At least one of us was getting some sleep.

I showered and dressed, and as I pulled my hair up into a messy bun, I realized that in all my panicking about Martin, I'd completely forgotten about another plausible suspect. Professor Omar from Richland University.

Both Eva and Martin had mentioned the man had visited Gunther's house. Martin had said he was expected that day. Was it possible that man was the killer?

It didn't seem likely. If Omar was planning to kill the man, he probably wouldn't have made an appointment. Certainly a professor was smarter than that.

Maybe they had argued, however. Maybe the killing wasn't planned.

Still not likely. What seemed more plausible was the possibility that the professor might be aware of an enemy who wanted Gunther dead.

If I could get that information from the professor, I wouldn't have to meet Martin.

I'd have to act fast, though.

First, I needed to find him. I grabbed my phone and typed in Professor Omar and Richland University.

The top listing in the search results was a faculty page for Dr. Abraham Omar, head of Richland University's archeology department. Bingo!

I clicked the link and found the professor's current course schedule and a brief biography, which highlighted the fact that he was a noted expert in ancient Egyptian history with experience leading digs in the Valley of the Kings and Luxor and had served in an advisory capacity on several other expeditions.

Impressive credentials, to be sure. No wonder Gunther relied on him. It also gave me hope that he was not killer material.

At the bottom of his faculty page was a phone number, so I called it. After a few rings, it went to voicemail, but the recording listed his office hours. Today's drop-in schedule was between seven and eight in the morning, which meant— I checked the time—yes, he should already be there. If I was quick, I could probably get there before he left.

I opened a can of tuna for Aneksi, who was still fast asleep. I picked her up, blanket and all, and left her in the bathroom with her food. If she had awoken, I would have apologized for abandoning her again, but she never even opened her eyes. I ran my fingers between her ears and whispered goodbye.

On my way out the door, I noticed Stirling's hat was still missing from the rack. Had he left early again? Or had he never come home?

Another, more troubling thought struck. Was he avoiding me?

Honestly, how could I blame him? When he invited his long-lost granddaughter to visit him, he probably wasn't counting on her facing a murder rap.

I couldn't think about that now, though. I had to get to the university within the hour. Luckily, it was less than a mile away. Still, by the time I found a place to park and his building, my hour was nearly up.

When I reached the professor's office door, I had only minutes to spare, and I was too frazzled to knock. Instead, I paused and took deep breaths to compose myself. When I was ready to knock, the door flew open. A young woman with a turquoise and purple braid trailing over one shoulder and a bulging messenger bag at her side pushed past me.

"Thanks, Professor. See you next week," she called back.

I peeked inside to find a hefty man squeezed behind a small desk in front of a bookcase that had books shoved into every conceivable space and at every conceivable angle. He didn't look up, but there was something familiar about that thick mass of black hair that brushed the collar of his linen blazer.

I knocked on the open door. "Excuse me, Professor Omar?"

When he faced me, my knees nearly buckled.

This was the man who had come into Cuthbert Exotic Antiques yesterday. The one who knew my name.

At the sight of me, he leaned back and tugged at his collar. "Rebecca Cuthbert? You aren't a student here."

I stood my ground despite every instinct screaming for me to leave. "I was hoping to speak with you about Gunther Vernon."

He grabbed a pile of manila folders off the desk and stood. "Now isn't a good time. You'll have to come back."

I pushed the door closed behind me so he couldn't leave. "I only need a minute."

His thick, angry eyebrows pulled together. "Excuse me?"

Was he trying to intimidate me? It wouldn't work. I was too desperate. This might be my only chance. "I was the one who found Mr. Vernon's body, and I understand you had an appointment to see him that afternoon."

He fumbled with his folders. "You must have me confused with somebody else. I don't—"

"That's what his domestic manager told the police. I've also spoken to Martin Fincher."

That stopped him. He glanced up, and we locked gazes. "What did Martin say?"

"That you've worked quite a bit with Mr. Vernon over the years."

"I have a number of clients who rely on my expertise to authenticate particular items."

"Like stolen artifacts?"

His frown carved a deep crevice between those bushy eyebrows. "As a general rule, I don't ask about the particulars."

"So, it's a don't-ask-don't-tell kind of situation?"

"I fail to see why this concerns you."

"Maybe it doesn't. But wouldn't Mr. Vernon have made some enemies in his line of work?"

"I'm sure he has."

"Do you know of any?"

"I really couldn't say."

"Couldn't or won't?"

"Potato, potahto."

This was getting me nowhere. I tried something else. "Eva Henriksen said he had a buyer for Cleopatra's cat. Do you know who it was?"

"Gunther did not share that information. No smart broker would."

His stare bored into me. I tried to think of something, anything to say. "Do you know of anyone with a grudge against Mr. Vernon?" I blurted. "Anyone who might wish to do him harm?"

"Good heavens, I hardly knew the man. I evaluated a few items he had acquired over the years, and that was the extent of our association."

I didn't need Adelaide Morris's investigative instincts to know he was lying. I could see it in that shifty gaze. He couldn't even look me in the eye. Instead, he fumbled with his folders.

"We both know that isn't true, sir. You were there to evaluate Cleopatra's cat, weren't you? Eva said you told him not to sell it."

He shrugged in a way that was neither a confirmation nor a denial. Then those dark eyes narrowed on me. "Would I be correct in believing this item is now in your possession? Or rather your grandfather's?"

"No, on both counts. Unfortunately, it was destroyed when Mr. Vernon was attacked."

Beneath his bushy mustache, his lips curled into a smirk. "You're lying."

"I'm not. I saw it. The pieces were all over the floor of Mr. Vernon's study."

The professor blanched. "It's unsealed?"

"If you mean broken, then yes. Did you know it was stolen?"

"No, he said he'd gotten it from..."

He didn't finish the sentence.

"It was stolen." As the man grew more defensive, my courage rallied. "From my grandfather's shop. I'll ask you again. Do you know who the buyer was? Or who attacked him?"

As he stared at me, I thought I could see an argument working through him. Was he about to tell me what he knew? No, he only tightened his grip on his folders, reached past me, and pulled open the door. He paused in the open doorway, and the look he gave me shook me to my core.

"If the vessel is truly broken," he said, "you have bigger problems, Miss Cuthbert. Much bigger problems, indeed."

CHAPTER TWENTY

Deadly Discovery

P ROFESSOR OMAR'S WARNING had me so rattled, I nearly panicked when I found the front door of Cuthbert Exotic Antiques unlocked. It was only nine, an hour before opening, and the lights were still off.

Fear washed over me.

Had someone broken in? Was a crime in progress?

After everything that had happened, I wasn't going to take any chances. I pulled my phone from my purse and dialed 91...

As my finger hovered over the button, I caught someone moving in the shadows at the back of the store. Was that the intruder? Was it a thief?

When a familiar bald head with silver glasses moved into the light, I knew it was neither.

It was Stirling.

The door jangled when I opened it and caught his attention.

"Rebecca, hello dear." He hardly glanced my way before

hurrying to the office. "I wasn't expecting you so early. Is everything all right?"

"I'm fine. Why is it so dark in here?"

There was a loud clunk and then a scraping sound, like something being dragged across the floor. Was he moving the desk? A cabinet? I hurried to help him do whatever it was he was doing, but he wasn't in the office. The sounds were coming from the storage closet.

When I pulled open the door, I found him leaning the broom and mop against the wall. He turned back with a guilty look.

"I came in to get a dust rag and managed to make quite a mess," he said. Once everything was back in place, he brushed off his hands and his shirtsleeves and pushed by me in a hasty exit.

"Aren't you missing something?"

He glanced back, and I handed him one of the microfiber towels.

"Right!" He grabbed it and chuckled. "Completely forgot what I went in there for."

When he ducked into the office instead of returning to the shop floor, I wondered if he was telling me the truth. I glanced around the small space, but nothing else seemed out of place. Could the mop and broom have made all that noise? It didn't seem likely. "Are you sure everything is all right?"

"Of course! What could be wrong?"

That was what I wanted to know. And if he was lying to me about this, which he clearly was, I had to wonder what else he was lying about.

Martin Fincher's warning echoed through me again.

Stirling placed the towel next to the kettle and stared at it for a long moment. "I'm glad you're here, Rebecca. There's something I'd like to say."

I braced myself. "All right."

"I owe you an apology."

Was this it? Was he going to come clean?

He clucked his tongue. "I'm afraid I've been taking advantage of you. You agreed to help in the shop, and I've all but abandoned you these past couple of days. That wasn't my intention. I've allowed myself to be pulled in so many directions, but I promise you, it ends today."

Was he telling me the truth? I searched his expression, but it told me nothing. "Don't worry about me. I'm fine."

At least that was the truth. I mean, I was fine. I liked spending time in the shop. Who wouldn't? All the history and mystery of an Adelaide Morris novel without the messy murders. Well, not as many murders, anyway.

He chuckled. "I hope you know I appreciate all you've done. You have been a bright light during a dark and trying time. I know it can't be easy, especially when you're dealing with such a profound loss."

I nodded, but for the first time in weeks, my grief wasn't foremost on my mind. The pain was still there, like fingers squeezing my heart, but it wasn't consuming every thought.

His hand slapped his forehead. "And this madness about Gunther Vernon. What is the name of that officer who was harassing you? I will be speaking to his superiors about that. It was completely out of line."

"It's all right. You don't have to." As much as I wished Stirling could make my troubles with the Citrus Grove Police Department disappear, that was my fight.

As long as we were clearing the air, I might as well do my part. "There's something I need to tell you, Stirling. I didn't mean to keep it from you, but…"

He straightened, bracing for what I'm sure he sensed was bad news. "What is it, my dear?"

"First, did you know Martin was working with Gunther Vernon?"

His expression didn't change, which told me he did.

He removed his glasses and pinched his nose before replacing them. "I suspected as much. I knew their paths had crossed at the university, but I never thought Martin would seek out the man's dubious services." He rubbed his face. "Unfortunately, it doesn't change anything. Was that what you wanted to tell me?"

"There's more. The detective said he couldn't find any record of the theft. His department lost the police report."

I expected him to be angry, but he didn't even look surprised.

"There's a good reason for that," he said. "I never actually filed a report. I know I probably should have, but Martin knew how to cover his tracks. The police wouldn't have found anything."

Was he serious? "But you told me you filed one."

"I know, and I'm sorry I misled you. In the end, I just didn't see the point."

He didn't see the point? "How did you expect to find Martin and get your property back? Not only that, the police would see it might be connected to what happened to Gunther. It might have given them more leads. As it stands, they're only looking at me, and I don't want to go to prison."

"You are not going to prison. I told you, I'll have a word with that officer's superior."

"He's a detective." It was hardly an important distinction under the circumstances, but my anger was taking over.

He held my gaze. "There are reasons I couldn't disclose what I knew about Martin and Gunther, and one day, I will share them with you. I'm sorry it cannot be today. But you must believe me, I will not let any harm come to you."

"How can you promise that? I doubt the police are going to ask your permission."

"It isn't something I'm presently at liberty to discuss."

So, he was keeping secrets. In a way, I was glad because I was still keeping one from him too. I couldn't tell him about Aneksi. He'd made his feelings about cats crystal clear, so there was a good chance—probably better than good—that he would force me to get rid of her if I told him.

I couldn't do that. At first, I'd told myself I didn't want to release her back to the streets because it wasn't safe for her. But that was only part of it. The truth was, I had become attached to that little creature. Hallucinations or not, I couldn't let her go. So, if I revealed her presence to my grandfather now, it would only lead to another argument, and I didn't want that. I also didn't have time for it because, like it or not, I had to go pick up Martin.

"Can we discuss this later?" I pulled my purse to my shoulder and turned toward the shop door.

"Where are you going?" he demanded. I could hear the worry in his voice.

Before I could answer, the shop's door swung open, and Detective Devon was in front of me.

His square jaw tensed. "You going somewhere, Miss Cuthbert?"

"Actually, I am." I wasn't interested in playing this game with him again. "If you'll excuse me."

When I tried to walk past him, he held out that tree trunk of an arm and stopped me. "I need to speak to you."

It took every ounce of self-control not to lose my temper. "Detective, is this really necessary?"

He replied with a question of his own. "Can you tell me where you were between seven and eight-thirty this morning?"

"I went to the university. I was there until about eight-thirty. Then I came back here."

He pulled out his notepad and a pen. "Can anyone corroborate that?"

I glanced at Stirling, who was watching from the doorway.

"Miss Cuthbert, can anyone corroborate that?" he repeated.

"I was with Professor Abraham Omar."

"You were what?"

Stirling's outburst startled me, but it seemed to take Detective Devon by surprise, too.

"What were you doing with Dr. Omar?" My grandfather inserted himself between me and the detective.

It was a straightforward question, but he wasn't going to like my straightforward answer. Still, there didn't seem to be any way around it. "Gunther had an appointment to see the professor the night he was killed. I went to talk to him about it."

"You don't even know that man. What makes you think they were working together?"

As Stirling fired questions at me, Detective Devon stood by, waiting for my answers.

"Does it matter?" I couldn't tell him the truth without making this interrogation a million times worse. Deflection seemed a safer option.

Stirling looked at Detective Devon with an expression that said *can you believe this?*

"Martin told me about him," I blurted.

The red flush that had been creeping up Stirling's neck engulfed his entire face. "You spoke to Martin Fincher? How did you manage that?"

Detective Devon's gaze darted back to me.

"Bitsie had his phone number. She was trying to help." I hoped I wasn't getting her in trouble. "She knew about Gunther, and she thought Martin might be able to help me clear my name. She was trying to help me." Which was more than he was doing, I wanted to point out.

Stirling was in no mood for my attempt at a guilt trip. "Why on earth would you be so reckless?" He was outright screaming now.

Detective Devon seemed to be getting hot around the collar, too. He stepped forward. "When did you speak with Mr. Fincher?"

"Yesterday, after the shop closed."

"What time exactly?" he pressed.

"Is it a crime to call someone now?"

"Miss Cuthbert." That mild irritation was creeping up on rage.

"Fine." I fished through my purse and pulled out my phone. I touched the screen and flipped through my call log. "I called him at 6:42 p.m. Look." I held the phone so he could read the time stamp for himself.

He scribbled on his notepad.

I shoved my phone back into my purse. "Why does it

matter?"

Stirling was running both hands over his freckled bald head.

Detective Devon, on the other hand, had settled into an icy glare. "I'll tell you why. A maid at the motel where Martin Fincher has been staying went to his room and found him this morning. Dead."

How was that possible? "Who killed him?"

If Detective Devon's gaze were a knife, it would have sliced me in half. "I was hoping you might be able to tell me."

That was when it dawned on me. He thought I did it. He was about to accuse me of another murder.

CHAPTER TWENTY-ONE

What Legacy?

DETECTIVE DEVON DROPPED his head back and stared at the ceiling. "I'm trying to keep an open mind, but you must see how bad this looks."

Of course I did, and my heart thundered in my chest so hard, I was afraid it would crack a rib. Any minute the detective was going to reach back for those handcuffs. "I can't help how it looks. All I can say is, I did not kill Martin Fincher. I didn't kill anyone. Check the security cameras at the university. They must have them. You'll see I was there."

Stirling was standing at my side, taking in every word. He stepped forward. "Where was Martin found?"

The detective rubbed his jaw before answering. "Chapman Motel. The manager on the premises said he checked in a few weeks ago."

Stirling frowned. "His apartment is less than a mile from there. He was hiding out, but he didn't go far. I wonder why that was."

"I can't speculate about that, but he was using a fake

name and paying cash. The motel manager also said he hardly ever left the room but was making dozens of phone calls a day. Any idea what he might have been up to?"

"Your guess is as good as mine, detective," Stirling said. "But what makes you say it was a homicide? Couldn't he have done himself in? Guilt can trigger such things, I hear."

"Funny you should mention that," the detective said, though he didn't look amused. "I think suicide is what the killer wanted us to believe."

The way the detective's gaze lingered on my grandfather, I wondered if we were now both suspects.

Martin's warning scratched again at the back of my mind. I'd believed Dr. Omar might be the monster Martin feared. I'd assumed the man had been on his way to teach a class, but could he have gone to Martin's instead? It seemed unlikely. Stirling was a different matter.

At the moment, there was only kindness and concern in my grandfather's deep, green eyes. He was a bit rumpled, a bit distracted, but hardly dangerous.

Or was it all an act?

I imagined that was the kind of thing Adelaide Morris would wonder, and it was a valid question. Everything about him could be an act.

Martin had asked me how well I knew my grandfather. I'd dismissed the question at the time, but the truth was, I didn't know him well at all.

Stirling lifted his chin and squared his shoulders. "Are

you here to make an arrest, detective?"

"Should I be?"

"I believe Rebecca and I have answered your questions. If there's nothing further, I'd say we're done here. Do you agree, Rebecca?" He looked at me.

"I've got nothing more to add," I said.

Detective Devon watched us both for what felt like an eternity, then smiled. "If you're involved, either of you, it would be better for you to cooperate now. I can't help you if you keep playing games."

"We're hardly playing games," Stirling groused. "We've told you what we know. Haven't we, Rebecca?"

"We have." I sounded less than convincing, even to my- self. "I wasn't anywhere near a motel, any motel. Call Professor Omar. He'll tell you."

He pulled out his notepad again. "Omar, right. Which department?"

"Archeology," I replied.

"I'll do that, then. Is there anything else you'd like to tell me before I go?" His gaze bounced from me to Stirling. "No?"

My grandfather stepped forward with his hand out, herd- ing Detective Devon toward the door. "If we can be of further assistance regarding this matter, please don't hesitate to call. We will be happy to answer any additional questions you may have. Won't we?" He glanced back at me.

"Absolutely. Any questions at all." I hung back as Stirling

directed the detective to the door, opened it, and all but pushed him through it.

Stirling watched our visitor from the window until he drove away. Only then did he turn around. "Why didn't you tell me you'd spoken to Martin?"

The heat in that question put me on the defensive. "I didn't think it was important." It wasn't a good excuse, but I couldn't think of anything else to say.

"It was foolish. You put yourself in danger. I'd never forgive myself if something happened to you. You must trust me on this."

"I told you, I thought he might know what happened to Gunther. I had to try. I don't want to go to prison."

"That will not happen. I can protect you, but you must trust me."

Trust him? Really? "How am I supposed to trust you? I don't even know where you are half the time."

His eyes flared. I braced for an outburst, but his anger subsided. "You're right," he said. "I haven't been honest with you. Perhaps it's time I start."

A thousand questions bounced around my brain. The scariest one slipped out. "Are you really my grandfather?"

I tried to decipher the look he gave me. Was it anger? Disappointment? Pain? I truly didn't know.

His chin dipped, and he clasped his hands behind his back. "Of course I am," he said solemnly. "But there's a reason your father never told you about me, or anything about the Cuthbert family legacy. I should have been honest with you about that from the start."

Now I was worried. "What legacy?" The shop? The stolen heirlooms? Something else entirely? My curiosity and dread grew in equal measure. "What do you mean?"

"His mother, your grandmother, left me when he was quite young. She didn't want him to have anything to do with me or the family business. After he was grown, he decided that's how he wanted to keep it. He turned his back on his roots long ago and never looked back." He went to the shop door, turned the sign to closed, pulled the shade down, and locked the door.

The confession frightened me, but him closing the shop out of the blue frightened me even more. It wasn't even noon.

"What are you doing?" Could he hear the tremble in my voice?

"There's something I'd like to show you. Will you come with me?" He ushered me to the back of the shop, toward the office.

Despite my trepidation, I did as he asked. But instead of going to the office, he stopped at the storage closet. He opened the door, flipped on the light, and stepped in beside the narrow metal shelf that held the cleaning supplies and an oscillating fan.

"Please come in." He offered his hand when he saw my confusion.

When I entered, he stepped back so his back was pressed firmly against the rack. "All the way, please. There's room. Yes, like that. Now, if you would close the door behind you."

This was beyond awkward. "Why?"

"Please," he urged.

I wanted to refuse, but he was adamant. I closed the door.

A sliver of light seeped in from the space between the door and the floor. It was enough that I could see him push aside the broom and the mop, then run his palms over the wood paneling. He seemed to be looking for something, and when he found it, he pressed.

That slight motion triggered a spring that popped the panel away from the wall.

I stared at it, hardly believing my eyes. "Is that a hidden door?"

CHAPTER TWENTY-TWO

The Warning

I'D BEEN IN the storage closet many times, yet I'd never noticed that hidden door. I peeked over Stirling's shoulder. "Where does that go?"

He stepped into the passage. "Follow me, and I'll explain."

It was too dark to see anything until Stirling grabbed a metal lever along the inside wall and pushed it upward. Naked light bulbs strung along the ceiling flickered to life, revealing a narrow staircase that descended to a lower room.

At the bottom, he flipped another switch, brightening more bulbs suspended down the middle of the room. It wasn't a large room, only about half the size of the shop above, yet it was difficult to say for sure because of all the stuff crammed down there. Old tables and chairs, rickety crates and lamps, and dozens of unopened crates.

"This reminds me of my parents' attic," I muttered, only half kidding. I didn't think my dad ever threw anything away.

"You never know when it might come in handy," he often said.

"Please, come this way." Stirling gestured for me to follow as he navigated through the stacks. He stopped when he reached a bare space along the rear concrete wall and looked back toward the staircase.

"Did you see something?" I asked.

"Just making sure we weren't followed. What I'm about to show you is our family's most important and closely guarded secret."

The seriousness in his expression gave me chills. "Why is it a secret?"

Instead of answering, he pushed aside a heavy, dusty drape, revealing a massive and imposing metal vault.

"What is that?" I reached out to touch the spindle at the center, but he nudged me back.

"Please allow me." He grabbed the spindle, spun it several full revolutions one way, then back, and then forward again. At the sound of a loud clank, he tugged on the handle, and the door slid open.

Inside was a space that was smaller than the one we were previously standing in but still a good-sized room, and it was unlike anything I'd ever seen. There were dusty wooden shelves edged with dull, metal rails. Scattered around were jewelry pieces, artifacts, and amulets that looked positively ancient, if the layer of dust covering them was any indication. But most of the shelves were empty, which made me think the stacks of dirty, cobweb-covered items on the floor must have tumbled from their places, and no one had bothered to put them back.

I entered behind Stirling and tried to make sense of the things I saw. An old chalice, tattered scrolls, a dusty turquoise and carnelian collar that was much larger and intricate than anything on the shop's shelves upstairs. I pointed to it. "Is that Egyptian?"

"It's all Egyptian," he said. "And ancient, by our standards, anyway. This is the Cuthbert Collection." There was an ominous tenor to his words that unsettled me.

"This all belongs to you?" I asked.

He scoffed lightly. "No, I would never presume to say anything here belongs to me or to anyone."

"But you called it the Cuthbert Collection?"

"I consider myself only to be a caretaker. A steward, you might say. As my father was before me, and his father before him. That is the Cuthbert Legacy. We take care of these items."

"Did my father know about all this?"

"He did." There was a world of sadness in those two words and that faraway gaze.

This was the legacy my father must have rejected when he abandoned his father.

I followed Stirling deeper into this secret room. Among the piles, I spotted a clay Sekhmet idol and a panpipe. So many strange and wondrous relics. What a shame they were left here, forgotten and buried in cobwebs.

He stopped at an empty space at the back of the room. He touched an empty place on a shelf. "This is where Cleopatra's cat stood."

When he walked away, I brushed the bare wood with my fingertips. I'd known it was precious to him, but now, seeing the honored place it once held, I felt the loss more keenly.

Stirling placed his palm on my shoulder. "I should have been a better caretaker. I neglected my duties. I know that now. For too long, I wanted to forget, and sometimes it was easy to do so. Perhaps that's why I became complacent. I don't know. I've gone over it in my mind a thousand times, and I still don't know. Yet somehow, Martin not only learned of this room, but he managed to enter it."

Even as I stood here, gazing upon these dusty, forgotten wonders, it still didn't make sense. "But why keep them here if they're so valuable? Shouldn't they be in a museum or a gallery?" I sounded like Eva Henriksen. Hadn't she made the same complaint about Gunther's collections?

Still, she had a point.

"They must remain hidden." He sighed and shook his head. "The items in this room have a dark and dangerous history." His eyes roamed the space. "I don't completely understand the power they hold. I only know my grandfather feared it and dedicated his life to protecting others from it."

"Protect? Do you mean they're cursed?" Martin's warning echoed through me again.

"Unfortunately, yes," Stirling said. "That is exactly what I mean." He must have seen my disbelief because he continued. "Cleopatra's cat, for instance. It was more than a statue. It was a funerary vessel."

"Like a coffin? For a cat?" I'd read about the Egyptians' practice of mummifying pets, but it still seemed odd.

"Yes, to put it bluntly. My grandfather believed it held one of Queen Cleopatra's pets, except the pet was not exactly deceased."

"That's horrible! It was buried alive?" People used to think slaves and servants were buried alive in the tombs of Egyptian pharaohs, but modern historians refuted the idea. Maybe it was the same here.

"J.P. Cuthbert believed it was true, only it was even more complicated," Stirling said. "The legend, which he discovered after the collection came into his possession, says that beloved cat was an immortal creature that could bestow immortality upon its master, or in the case of Cleopatra, its mistress. Some believed, as he did, that it was the secret to her enduring youth and vitality, which the men of her acquaintance seemed to find so alluring."

I waited for him to flash a smile, like this was a joke. But there was no smile or amusement of any kind in his expression.

Still, none of it made sense. "So, Cleopatra's cat was a vessel for a mummified cat? But I saw the broken pieces.

There was nothing inside."

"I hope that's true. But I fear whatever magic was contained within it could now be unleashed upon the world."

That was a terrifying thought.

He touched my shoulder, and his steely gaze locked on mine. "I'm afraid whoever killed Gunther knew about that magic and wanted it for themselves. Perhaps that person has become so desperate, they've killed again. They may have believed the creature was still in Martin's possession. The poor boy. I'm sure he had no idea what he was getting himself into when he entered this room."

My grandfather took my hands in both of his. "I didn't want to tell you this way, but you have a right to know. You might already be in danger because of it. One day—"

A red light flashed over the door and stopped him. His eyes went wide with alarm.

"What is that?" I asked.

"A warning," he said. "Someone's broken into the shop."

CHAPTER TWENTY-THREE
Next Door Dilemma

S TIRLING PUT HIS finger to his lips and waved me back, silently telling me to stay behind him as he ascended the staircase to the storage closet to see who had triggered the alarm.

When he opened the door, I peered over his shoulder and saw Professor Omar prowling through the shop, yelling for my grandfather.

"Omar, of course," Stirling muttered. He whispered back to me, "Stay here. I'll take care of this."

I inched back but kept the door open slightly to watch Stirling approach the gruff professor. "What's the meaning of this?"

The larger man whipped around when he heard my grandfather. "If you intend to close early, you should probably lock the door, Stirling."

They were on a first-name basis?

"Thank you for the tip, old friend, though I distinctly remember doing so," my grandfather replied in a less than friendly tone. "I thought we had an understanding?"

"Of course we do. But, I thought you should know Gunther—"

Stirling cut him off with a raised hand. "Let's discuss this in my office. I feel the need for some tea. Would you mind starting the kettle while I lock the door? The office is to the right."

"I remember," the brutish man growled back.

I pulled farther into the shadow as Professor Omar entered the hallway before disappearing into the office. After Stirling secured the shop's front door, he followed the man into the office.

He closed the door behind himself.

Why would he do that? I could think of only one reason. He didn't want me to overhear their conversation.

That creepy, crawly feeling came over me again. He'd already told me—and shown me—his big secret. But there must be more.

What else was he hiding?

Was *he* the killer? Was the professor?

My mind exploded with fresh doubts and fears. I didn't know what to think, but I knew this—the answer to my questions was behind that door.

I knew what Adelaide Morris would do if she were in my place, or rather what she wouldn't do. She wouldn't hide in a storage room. She'd find a way to listen in. Keyholes were especially handy in her situations, but Stirling's door didn't have one.

Maybe a glass on the door? It might work, but the only glasses we had in the shop were in the office with him.

Then it struck me. There might be another way.

I slipped from my hiding place as silently as I could and hurried out the back door. Once I was at our neighbor's door, I knocked as hard as I could.

"Bitsie, did you lose your key again? You can't keep—" Luna stopped when she opened the door and saw me. "Sorry, I thought you were Bitsie. Is something wrong?"

"I need your help."

She must have sensed my panic because she searched the alley in one direction and then the other. "What happened? Are you all right? Is someone bothering you?" She stepped back, waved me inside, and looked me over. "Are you hurt?"

There wasn't time to explain, so I got to the point. "Can I see that secret room you found?"

She frowned. It obviously wasn't the question she was expecting. "I guess so. Any particular reason? Did you tell Stirling?"

"No, I didn't say anything. But I need to check something." I hurried by her to get to the room. I hoped it wasn't already too late. "It's here, isn't it?"

"Yes, there. On the right."

Mentally, I tried to picture the two floor plans, side by side. I hoped I was right.

When I reached the door, I paused. "Is Bitsie inside?"

"No, she went to Malone's to grab a sandwich. I expect her back any minute. Are you sure you're all right?"

No, I wasn't. What I really needed was a friend, someone who could tell me if I was making a mountain out of a molehill. Bitsie was the closest thing I had to that in Citrus Grove.

What I did have, however, was Luna Sage, even if she was looking at me like I should be fitted for a straitjacket.

"I'm worried about Stirling," I blurted. "There's a man at the shop, and I think he's dangerous."

That got her attention. "How dangerous?"

"I'm not sure. They're talking in the office with the door closed. I need to hear what they're saying. I need to know if he's threatening my grandfather."

Luna looked slightly relieved. "He's probably a vendor. Bitsie works with some sketchy ones, too. They're usually not as scary as they look."

"He's not a vendor." I probably should have told her more, but this was already taking too much time. I needed to get inside that room.

"Why do you think he's in danger?"

Why was she so nosy? But then, who was I to talk? And she was the ex-girlfriend of Stirling's thieving ex-manager, who was now also dead. She probably knew the professor. She probably knew a lot more than she was letting on.

"I don't know," I said, cautiously. "I just want to know if he's threatening Stirling. If he is, I'm calling the police."

"You aren't kidding, are you?" Her smile faded. "Poor Stirling! How can I help? What do you need?"

I wasn't expecting that. Maybe Bitsie was right about this woman after all. "Right now, I want to get in that room. I think it shares a wall with Stirling's office. Do you have a glass?"

She stepped into the shop's office and returned with a small drinking glass. Perfect!

I grabbed it from her and ducked into the room. I put the open end on the unfinished wall facing what I hoped was Stirling's office and put my ear to the other end. There were mumblings, but nothing I could understand.

Luna had grabbed her own glass and took a spot next to me. As she did, she nudged a large box to make more space.

Suddenly, the voices were louder.

When I looked to see why, I noticed the box she had moved had been covering a vent in the wall. That vent apparently connected to Stirling's office. Success!

Instantly, I heard the professor's raspy whisper.

"You know what must be done," he said ominously.

Stirling mumbled something I couldn't decipher.

"It didn't have to come to this," the professor added. "You should have been honest with me. Now, you leave me no choice."

I looked at Luna, and she looked at me. She mouthed, *a threat?* I shrugged an I-don't-know, but I'm sure the look on my face told her I feared the worst.

The professor kept talking. "It's all very unfortunate," he grumbled. "Don't you agree? We have to end this."

End what? I didn't know, but the look on Luna's face told me she was thinking the same awful thing I was. Stirling was definitely in danger.

Without thinking twice, I scrambled out of that room and back to the alley. But what was I going to do? There was no way I could overpower that beast of a man.

When I threw open the back door to Stirling's shop, I still didn't have a plan, but it didn't matter. The professor had one hand on my grandfather's shoulder and the other was shutting the shop's front door behind them.

I ran to catch up, but when I reached the door, I saw the professor was settling into the driver's seat of an old Volvo parked in front of the shop. In the seat beside him was my grandfather, bent forward with his head in his hands.

I was too late. That fiend had Stirling.

CHAPTER TWENTY-FOUR

Trouble, Fur Sure

"WHERE ARE THEY going?"

Luna's question startled me. I hadn't realized she'd followed me, but here she was, standing beside me at the shop window, watching the professor drive away with my grandfather.

"I wish I knew. I think Stirling's in trouble, though."

"Then what are you waiting for?"

At first, I wasn't sure what she meant. But then it hit me. "You're right," I sputtered. "I have to go after him. Will you lock up for me?" I fished the shop key out of my pocket and handed it to her.

She pulled back. "I meant call the cops."

"There's no time." I pressed the key into her hand and ran out before she could stop me.

As I unlocked my car door, a tuft of gray cat hairs clinging to my sleeve stopped me. Aneksi. It was the second day I'd left her alone in that bathroom. Once was bad. Twice was just cruel.

Not only that, I had a strong suspicion that she was more than a feral kitten who had randomly made her way into my car. If my suspicion was right, she was the immortal pet entombed in that funerary vessel. It would explain why she'd been in such poor shape when I found her and why she'd improved so quickly, as if by magic.

She *was* magic.

Maybe deep down I'd suspected that all along, but it was just too bizarre to believe.

But I couldn't deny it any longer. Doing so would only put that sweet little furball in greater danger because, if Stirling was right about the killer, that person was searching for her. At the moment, my gut was saying that person was Professor Omar, and that he'd probably taken Stirling back to Gunther's house to search for the cat.

When they didn't find her there, it would be only a matter of time before Omar would want to search Stirling's apartment, which meant I had to get her out of there.

I relocked my car and dashed to Stirling's apartment.

When I opened the bathroom door, I was still debating where to take her. "Aneksi? Sweetie, you need to come with me."

She uncurled herself from the pale-blue rug in front of the sink and sat up with a curious expression. "Where have you been?"

The question no longer surprised me. I still wasn't sure I believed everything Stirling had said about her being an immortal creature with otherworldly powers, but I knew there was something special about her. I also knew our conversations were not figments of my imagination. She wasn't a hallucination. She was my friend, and I had to protect her.

The last thing I wanted to do was worry her, though, so I kept the business about a killer on the loose to myself.

"I'll explain on the way." I grabbed her around the middle as delicately as I could and hoisted her into my arms.

She nudged the top of her head against my shoulder. "Why are your cheeks pink? Your heart is pounding. Are you ill?"

"Not exactly. It's complicated, but you might be in danger."

Her head craned back and those sparkling blue eyes gazed up at me. "I have sensed no danger."

I slanted her a glance. "So, you're clairvoyant, too? Wait, never mind. Let's focus on one problem at a time. Right now, we need to get you out of here."

But where was I going to take her?

Detective Devon sprang to mind. If I told him everything, he would protect her. Then a vision of what that conversation would look like flashed through my mind.

Me: I know you think I killed a guy, maybe two, but there's this other bad guy who just kidnapped my grandfather and he might also want to hurt my new cat. Oh, and he's probably after her because she can talk and she's immortal. In fact, she might have been Cleopatra's pet.

Ugh. If I said any of that, he'd throw me behind bars in a red-hot second. Or at least send for a straitjacket.

But if I didn't tell him about Aneksi's unique qualities, why would he help her?

The short answer was, he wouldn't.

That left me with one last option, and if I was lucky, she'd be back in her shop by now.

I reached up and scratched Aneksi behind the ears. "Will you do me a favor?"

She lifted a tired gaze at me. "I will not like it, will I?"

"Probably not, but it's for your own good."

"Very well. What is it?"

A FEW MINUTES later, I hurried out of the lobby of Heritage View Apartments with my purse cradled to my chest because Aneksi was tucked snugly inside. I'd removed everything from the bag to make it as comfortable as possible—my wallet, my hairbrush, hand lotion, makeup bag, miniature sewing kit, emergency chocolate, and a travel-size tissue pack. My driver's license, a credit card, and keys were stuffed into the front pocket of my jeans.

"How are you doing?" I whispered as I walked briskly along the sidewalk.

"Please stop bouncing. It is upsetting my stomach."

"Sorry." I slowed my pace but only a little. "Better?"

"Some. How far away is your friend?"

"We're nearly there." The friend I'd told her about was Bitsie, who I hoped would be back from getting sandwiches at Malone's. She was the only cat lover I knew in Citrus Grove, and the closest thing to a friend I had who might be willing to catsit on the spot. Once she set eyes on this furry ball of cuteness, I hoped she'd be too enamored to ask questions. "Bitsie will watch over you while I search for Stirling. But you have to act like a normal cat. Can you do that?"

"By normal, I assume you mean silent."

I still wasn't quite used to her unnerving Miss Marple tone. "Exactly. No talking. Can you do that?"

"*Mee-Yow.*"

Even muffled, her displeasure was obvious. "Not ideal, I know. But it's our only option."

"Does this human have tuna?"

As I pulled open the shop door and brushed by a coyly smiling Elvis cardboard cutout, I searched for the platinum-haired woman. I didn't see her, but at the back of the store, I noticed the ice cream sign with the flavors posted. Cats liked milk, didn't they? Maybe she'd like ice cream. "I'm sure she'll find something."

"Rebecca, you're back! Did you find Stirling?" Luna popped out from behind a display case of Marilyn Monroe music boxes with a rag in one hand and spray cleaner in the other.

"Not yet. Is Bitsie here?"

She shook her head. "I'm starting to get worried, too. She's not usually gone this long without checking in."

Oh no. My plan was already falling apart. I leaned against the counter to regroup, but Aneksi chose that moment to stretch and rearrange herself inside my purse.

Luna's forehead wrinkled. "Did your purse just move?"

I tightened my grip on it. "It did. That's why I'm here. I was hoping Bitsie might do me a favor, but … well, I need a cat sitter."

"You have a cat in there?" Luna leaned forward. "Can I see it?"

Maybe Bitsie wasn't the only cat lover I knew. "Absolutely! Can I leave her with you? I won't be gone long." Honestly, I had no idea how long it would take to find Stirling, or even if it was possible, but I was beyond desperate.

Luna started to shake her head when a furry gray head emerged from my purse. Aneksi directed her wide, blue eyes at my new friend, and she meowed a very convincing meow.

Luna's face brightened. "Aww! She is adorable. Can I pet her?"

I was going to caution against it, but it was too late. Luna already had her hand on Aneksi's head. The cat didn't seem to mind. She closed her eyes and purred. "I think you've won her over."

"She's such a beauty. What's her name?"

"Aneksi."

"Never heard that one before. I'll bet there's a story behind it."

She had no idea.

"It just came to me." I hoped I wasn't insulting my feline friend.

Luna considered that sweet, furry face. "It's a great name. Sounds majestic, like an ancient goddess or something."

Aneksi stretched and preened, which I assumed meant she approved.

Luna sank her hands deep into the bag and pulled the cat out. "Go do whatever you need to do. I'll keep her in the back. I'm sure Bitsie won't mind. Did you bring any food for her?"

Food? Why hadn't I remembered to bring something? "She had some tuna this morning. Maybe she'd like some ice cream. I'll pay for it."

"Does she drink milk? You know, despite what many people think, most cats are lactose intolerant."

"I didn't know that." Guess it was a good thing Stirling hadn't had any in the fridge.

Luna pulled Aneksi close to her chest and cuddled her, which Aneksi allowed. "I'll figure out something. We'll be fine. Won't we, Aneksi?"

There was another convincing meow.

"You're a lifesaver, Luna. Thank you." I scratched Aneksi

between the ears and bent down to look her in the eye. "Please be good while I'm gone."

Aneksi meowed again and winked.

CHAPTER TWENTY-FIVE
Sarcasm and Suspicion

DETECTIVE DEVON STARED at me like I had lost my mind. "What do you mean Professor Omar kidnapped your grandfather? They were just here, and your grandfather did not appear to be under duress."

"They were here?" That didn't make sense. If the professor had killed Gunther and Martin, and possibly planned to kill Stirling, why would he go to the police station?

Was he setting me up?

"What were they doing here?" I demanded.

"You know I can't tell you that. It's police business."

"But he has my grandfather. I overheard them talking. He was definitely threatening Stirling."

"How so?"

"He said, 'You know what must be done,' and that kind of thing." Even as I repeated the words, I realized they didn't sound so bad. "It was more the way he said it. It was menacing."

"I see. And you were in the shop with them when he said

this?"

"Sort of. Well, no, not exactly."

"Where were you?"

Should I tell him I was eavesdropping from the shop next door? Was that illegal?

"Miss Cuthbert, where were you?"

He could be so frustrating. Why was he focusing on me when my grandfather was in danger? The way he was staring, I knew he would hound me until I answered. "I was next door. The shops share a vent. You can hear things."

My confession earned a look of mild surprise. "You were eavesdropping, and this is what you think you heard?"

"*Think* I heard? No, it's what I did hear. Are you going to help me find my grandfather or not?"

That gruff exterior softened. "I know your heart is in the right place, but you have to trust me. He didn't appear to be in danger."

"Why were they here?"

"They were here to discuss police matters. That's all I'm at liberty to say."

He really was the worst. "People have died, detective. I told you Martin Fincher was working with Gunther Vernon, and Gunther was working with Professor Omar. That's a pretty big coincidence, don't you think?"

He shook his head. "It doesn't matter what I think, Miss Cuthbert. It's what the evidence will prove, and you have no evidence to support your claim. What you have is merely conjecture."

"The evidence is that…" I sighed. I didn't have any, and he knew it.

"I suggest you let me do my job."

He had a point, but I wasn't going to back down. "You've hauled me in for questioning and made it clear I'm a suspect. Why won't you even consider that man could be involved? He knew and worked with both victims, which is more than you can say about me."

Detective Devon remained cool. Too cool, if anyone asked me. Then, to my surprise, he nodded. "You're right. We're well aware of Professor Omar's associations. But you're wrong if you think we didn't consider him a suspect. He very much was a suspect. Not that it's any concern of yours."

"He was?"

"Yes. *Was.* I've interviewed him, and I checked out his alibi. Did you know he livestreams his classes as part of the university's virtual program? He was either lecturing or preparing to lecture at the time of both murders. There are about two hundred students scattered across the country who can attest to his whereabouts."

A lanky young man in a lab coat approached Detective Devon's desk and flipped through the pages of a clipboard until he got the detective's attention.

"Do you have something for me?"

The younger man's gaze popped up. "Oh, sorry to interrupt, but the tests you ordered came back. I thought you'd want to know your hunch was right. Botulism toxin in both cases. Lethal doses of it, which is really surprising because—"

He clearly had more to say, but the detective stopped him with a gesture. "Thank you. I'll take the report."

"Right." The technician pulled a few sheets from the clipboard and handed them over. "It's all in there."

"I appreciate it." The look the detective gave him made it clear the younger man was dismissed.

When he was out of earshot, I said, "He's talking about Gunther and Martin, isn't he?"

I wasn't sure until the detective sucked in his cheeks and looked away. "It's police business, Miss Cuthbert."

"But I saw Gunther. He wasn't poisoned. His head was bleeding, like he was hit there. Hard."

"One doesn't necessarily negate the other."

"He was hit on the head *and* poisoned?"

"It would appear so."

That killer wasn't leaving anything to chance. "And Martin?"

"Poisoned."

"Wait. Isn't botulism just a fancy way of saying food poisoning? Can it really kill somebody?"

"A lethal dose can and pretty quickly, too."

My mind raced, trying to fit the new information into this mental jigsaw puzzle. "Doesn't that make the professor a more likely suspect?"

"How do you figure?"

"He works at the university. He must have access to the science labs."

"In the archeology department? We're not talking King Tut's curse here."

"He might work in the archeology department, but I'm sure he could get into the university's science labs, if he tried."

"Doubtful."

This man was so aggravating. "Why won't you even consider it? Is it because you want to pin it on me?" Anger was probably obscuring my judgment, but none of this seemed reasonable.

"There's more to it," he said. "The kind of botulism we found you wouldn't find it in a college laboratory. Trust me. He isn't our guy."

Trust him? Not likely. I could feel my composure slipping away, but I didn't care. "I think you're wrong, and I think you're making a huge mistake. Stirling is in danger, and if anything happens to him because you're giving this guy a free pass, I'm never going to forgive you."

"I'm sorry you feel that way."

The way he bent his head to the side and looked at me, really looked at me, made me want to believe him.

Nope. I wasn't falling for that. I had to get out of here before I said something I'd regret.

I stood, ready to leave. "Thank you for your time. I'll let

you get back to work." I bolted down the aisle.

When he said my name, I stopped and turned back.

There was still that wistful look in his eyes that made me a little weak in the knees. He gave me a half-smile and said, "You're free to go, but don't go far. You're still a suspect."

CHAPTER TWENTY-SIX

Mayhem at the Diner

DETECTIVE DEVON'S WORDS were still echoing through me as I maneuvered my car out of the police station's parking lot. So much for getting his help. He didn't believe my grandfather even needed help.

The only silver lining was I'd learned how the murderer had killed both victims. Botulism seemed an odd choice. The only serious case of botulism poisoning I'd ever encountered involved a neighbor who landed in the hospital after eating from a bad batch of home-canned tomatoes.

Wait a minute. Canned tomatoes? My stomach did a flip-flop as one thought led to another. Maybe I was wrong about the professor.

Instead of pulling into a parking spot near my grandfather's shop, I took an extra turn around the traffic circle and headed back to Malone's Diner. If the killer was poisoning his victims with a botulism toxin, I had a pretty good idea where it came from.

Unfortunately, it also meant the killer had been under

my nose the entire time.

I pulled into an open parking spot across the street from the restaurant, so I could watch Hank through the plate-glass window. He was doing what he usually did. Taking orders and carrying platters of food from the kitchen to the customers. I had to admit, he had me fooled. I might not have put it together if I hadn't seen that bag on Gunther's desk.

It would be so easy for Hank to contaminate Gunther's order with bacteria from that science experiment growing in his cabinet, then finish him off once the poison started to work its way through his system. Why Hank would want to kill that man wasn't as obvious, but it had to have something to do with Luna. Was he killing off a romantic rival? Or had Luna asked him to do it? Were the two of them working together?

My mind raced through possibilities, but if I'd learned anything from my failed visit to the police station, it was that theories weren't going to get me anywhere with that detective. I needed solid evidence.

That meant I needed to get that can of moldy fuzz into the detective's hands, or I would remain his number-one suspect.

I dialed the detective's number, expecting to get his voicemail. Instead, he picked up on the first ring.

"I'm sorry to bother you," I said, "but could you meet me at Malone's Diner?"

He didn't answer at first, then slowly and a bit awkwardly he said, "Thank you, but I've already eaten. Maybe another time."

Why was he being so weird? Then it dawned on me, and my cheeks flushed. "I'm not asking you on a date." The way I blurted those words probably made me look even guiltier, but it was too late to recover. "What I mean is, I know … I think I know … forget it. Please, just come. 'Bye."

I clicked the button to end the call and stared blankly at my phone. What had I done? I mean, besides make a complete fool of myself.

I shoved the phone back into my purse, lifted my chin, and reminded myself what was at stake. Justice, and a future that didn't involve orange jumpsuits. Once I found that jar and set the record straight, the detective would understand I was only trying to prove my innocence and that I didn't want to date him.

Because I didn't. The guy wasn't even my type. He was arrogant and rude, and if his desk was any indication, very messy, too.

Why was I even thinking about him? I needed to focus on getting into the diner's back room so I could get that can.

When I entered the restaurant, a booth was occupied by a pair of young women staring into laptops, sipping from bowl-sized coffee cups, and nibbling on giant muffins.

"Hey, Rebecca. I'll be with you in a jiffy." Hank was standing over a back table, wiping it down with a rag.

I waved and tried to look natural. *He doesn't know why*

you're really here. "Thanks. No rush."

I settled onto the stool closest to the swinging kitchen door, grabbed a menu, and tried to read it. The surge of adrenaline pumping through me made it impossible.

When he came to the counter, he grabbed the coffee carafe. "Can I get you a cup? It's fresh." He lifted it to his nose and sniffed. "Relatively."

It didn't inspire confidence. "Could I get a cup of hot tea instead?" I tried to smile and prayed he couldn't hear the pounding in my chest.

He grabbed one of those huge coffee mugs and filled it with steaming hot water. He set it in front of me with a small dish of assorted teas. "Today's special is meatloaf sandwich. It's Stirling's favorite."

Stirling. How did he figure into Hank's plan? "Have you seen him today?" I tried to keep my tone light, so he didn't suspect I was onto him as I unwrapped a minty black tea.

"He hasn't been in yet, which is odd." His eyebrows pulled together. "Is everything all right with him? He hasn't seemed like himself lately."

Interesting question. It reminded me how the villains in Adelaide Morris's mysteries sometimes tried to deflect their own guilt onto others. Was he trying to manipulate me the same way? I tried to play along. "It's been a difficult time for him, you know. Losing his son, obviously, and the theft at the store. And now Martin's death."

I studied Hank's expression, searching for signs of guilt.

The guy's jaw tensed as he watched the cars passing outside. "Understandable, I guess, but Martin ripped him off. Not sure why he'd be broken up about that. Pretty unforgivable, if you ask me."

Interesting. He sounded like someone who knew something about unforgivable acts. "I suppose you're right." I pulled a packet of raw sugar from the tray on the counter and emptied it into the cup with the steeping tea bag. "Do you think he got what he deserved?"

"Maybe so." He glanced at the clock over the kitchen pass-through window, then back at me. "Will you excuse me?" He whirled around before I could answer and darted down the corridor that led to the customer restrooms.

Had I struck a nerve? I didn't know, but when he disappeared around the corner, I knew it was my opportunity. I hopped off the stool and approached the round window embedded in the kitchen door. I peeked inside to see if anyone was there. The coast looked clear, so I pushed through and skirted the edge of the stainless-steel prep table until I made it to the back storage room, where I'd seen that moldy jar.

When I reached the spot, the thing was gone. I scoured the area around it, even the adjacent shelves. Still nothing. I worked my way down the line, pushing aside the stacks of napkins and bundles of paper towels, extra boxes of utensils and paper cups. Every jar of tomato sauce was gone.

"What are you doing in here?"

Hank's question paralyzed me. Slowly, I turned around, trying desperately to think of an excuse. "I was looking for…" My gaze landed on a stack of folded dish towels, and I grabbed one. "I needed a towel. I spilled some tea on my shirt, and I didn't think you'd mind. Do you mind?" I rubbed a corner of the towel on my sleeve and inched toward the door.

His eyes narrowed.

The bell on the diner's door jangled. The college students were leaving. My heart dropped. I hadn't seen any other customers or staff.

The realization sank in slowly. I was alone with Hank.

Would he try to kill me, too?

"Funny," he said in a way that wasn't funny at all, "you didn't strike me as the type. But I can assure you, there's nothing worth stealing in here."

"I'm not stealing!" I had braced for an attack but not on my character. Before I could even make sense of what he thought I was doing, a figure appeared behind him.

When I recognized Detective Devon, I nearly fainted with relief.

He slapped Hank on the back with one hand, while the other held the grip of his holstered service revolver. "Hey, big guy. I can take it from here."

"Perfect timing," Hank growled. "I found her ransacking the place."

"I wasn't ransacking anything," I shot back. "I was looking for your homemade botulism. Or should I say, murder weapon. I know it was you. You cultivated that poison to kill Gunther, and then you killed Martin with it. That's why I called Detective Devon. Go on, detective, arrest him. He is your killer."

Hank's face flamed red. "You think I killed those people? That's insane."

"Then you deny hiding that moldy jar of muck and fuzz back here?" I demanded.

"No, I'm not denying it, but I was not—how did you put it?—cultivating poison. It was a stupid mistake. I didn't even know it was there until Gil discovered it when he was back here washing dishes. We deep clean the kitchen and the pantry top to bottom every night, but we don't usually keep food in here. It's only for extra storage."

Detective Devon scratched his head. "How did a moldy jar wind up back here then?"

Hank pinched the bridge of his nose and shook his head. "It had to be the day I brought my dad back here a couple weeks ago. His nurse needed to pick her son up at school because he was sick, and I couldn't leave my dad home alone. When he got here, he wanted to help. I figured he couldn't do much harm back here washing dishes, but he got it into his head to start rearranging some things. I've been finding surprises all over the place. He gets confused sometimes, but he won't admit it, so we just deal with it. This was one of those times. I thought we'd found all his mistakes but apparently not."

"I'm sorry to hear about Big Hank," Detective Devon said softly.

Hank stared at his feet. "You aren't going to turn this over to the health inspectors, are you?"

The detective looked like he was considering it, then shook his head. "It wasn't in the kitchen. There's no food stored back here, so I don't see how there could be any cross-contamination."

"Thanks," Hank said. "You know how seriously we take that kind of thing."

"Wait a minute," I demanded. "How do you know he's telling the truth? Two people are dead from botulism, and he was growing it right here. He even admits it!"

Hank reeled back. "Hold on. I admit that jar being left out was a mistake, a horrible mistake, but it wasn't on purpose. I definitely wasn't trying to hurt anyone. I didn't like Martin because of the way he treated Luna, but I would never hurt him or Gunther Vernon. I barely knew that guy."

"Then why did you lie about him coming in here?" I demanded. "You pretended like you didn't even know who he was when I asked you about him yesterday."

He closed his eyes and shook his head. "You're right. I pretended I didn't know him because I didn't like him. I've never liked him or that bossy woman who works for him. I certainly never liked Martin Fincher. But I wasn't trying to hide anything, I just didn't have anything nice to say so I figured it was best to say nothing at all."

"That's awfully convenient," I sniped.

"Are you trying to accuse me of murder?" He turned to Detective Devon. "She can't do that, can she? That's libel."

The detective shook his head. "Maybe slander, but definitely not libel." He turned back to me. "So, this is why you wanted me to come down here? So you could make false accusations against Hank?"

"They aren't false. He obviously hated Martin. That's a motive. He had botulism growing right here in his restaurant, and I saw a Malone's bag at Gunther's house. Don't you find that suspicious?" Why were they both staring at me with looks of pity?

"Hello? Hank, are you back there?"

Hank leaned back. "In here, Luna."

Detective Devon stared at the ceiling like he was trying not to lose his patience. He stepped aside when Luna joined him at the doorway.

"What's going on?" She looked at each of us, puzzled. "Did I miss something?"

Hank gestured at me. "Your new friend thinks I'm a killer. She's trying to get me arrested."

"Nobody is getting arrested." Detective Devon stepped forward with his hands up. "This is all a misunderstanding."

"No, it isn't," I argued.

He turned a disgusted look my direction. "Yes. It is. Like I told you before, it was not that kind of botulism. And now you're trespassing. I think you need to go home and give that overactive imagination of yours a rest before it gets you into trouble."

"What do you mean, go home?" Hank demanded. "Aren't you going to arrest her for trespassing back here?"

"C'mon, Hank. No real harm was done," the detective said in a more soothing tone. "Her heart was in the right place. Emotions are running high, but we're all just trying to see that justice is done. Luna, could you see that Rebecca gets home safely?"

She looked at Hank first. He nodded, grudgingly.

"Sure, I can do that," she said. "C'mon, Rebecca. Let's get out of here."

I stared at her outstretched hand. My head was still spinning. I didn't want to leave. What I wanted was for the detective to believe me. He was right about one thing, though. I wanted justice, and this didn't feel like it.

Detective Devon watched me, then he put his hand behind his back. I heard the clink of him removing his handcuffs from his pocket.

He wouldn't dare. Would he? I grabbed Luna's hand. "Fine, I'm going. But I want it on the record that I think this is a huge mistake."

CHAPTER TWENTY-SEVEN
Missing

LEAVING MALONE'S DINER was the last thing I wanted to do, but Detective Devon's mind was made up. Whether I was wrong about Hank or not, there was still Stirling to consider. Was Hank conspiring with Professor Omar? It didn't seem likely, but so many unlikely things had happened since I'd arrived in Citrus Grove. I wasn't going to rule it out.

But with Malone's now off limits and no idea where the professor had taken my grandfather, I wasn't sure what to do next.

Luna and I were crossing the street as we walked back to the shop when she broke the uneasy silence between us.

"The detective's right about Hank. I've known him a long time. He wouldn't hurt anyone. It's not in him."

"You might think so, but people can surprise you." People like best friends and fiancés who can lie to your face without you even knowing it. "But right now, that's the detective's problem. I need to find my grandfather. I've lost too many people. I can't lose him, too."

The sad smile she gave me told me she understood, which I wasn't expecting, considering I'd just accused her boyfriend of murder. "Where will you look?"

"I don't know." I was toying with the idea of returning to the professor's university office, but even if something incriminating was there, the door would probably be locked.

No wonder Adelaide Morris had learned to pick them.

As we passed Heritage View Apartments' main door, Luna paused. "Do you want to go upstairs for a while? A nap might do you some good. I know I have a hard time doing anything when I'm tired. We can keep an eye on Aneksi for you."

I'd completely forgotten about the cat. Panic struck me. "Wait. If you're here, who's watching Aneksi now?"

"Bitsie came back. She's with her."

"Is she behaving herself? Aneksi, I mean. Not Bitsie."

"When I left, she was curled up on a blanket in the office, sleeping like an angel."

That was a relief. Still, I wanted to collect her before she overstayed her welcome. Luna followed close behind.

I was the first to reach their shop door. When I tried to open it, it was locked. The closed sign hung in the window. I spun around to Luna. "I thought Bitsie was back."

Luna looked as confused as I was.

Had something happened to them? Had the killer found her?

Luna fished a ring of keys from her purse and opened the door. "Bitsie, are you here?"

No one answered.

"Maybe she's in the office. Sometimes she locks the door when she's working back there." She led the way to a back room that contained a desk with a computer and a few file cabinets. Along the back wall was a blanket folded on the floor. No Aneksi.

"Maybe Bitsie took her for a walk?" Luna said.

"Cats don't go for walks."

"Right. Well, they have to be close by. I mean, where would they go?" Luna was trying to sound calm, but I could see the worry in her eyes.

"Did she leave a note?"

Luna perked up. "Yes! She probably left a note. She always leaves notes." She went to the desk and sifted through several piles of paper. If Bitsie had left anything there, it would be impossible to find in that mess. While Luna searched, I checked the back counter.

"What's this?" I pointed to a large box next to the printer.

Luna glanced over her shoulder. "That's more stuff Bitsie brought back from Mexico."

I pulled up the cardboard flaps to peek inside. It was mostly vintage plates and newspaper-wrapped figurines. In one corner, beside a pair of Elvis salt and pepper shakers, a white acrylic box looked out of place. I pulled it out.

Inside were seven tiny medical vials lined up in two tidy rows, with three empty slots where vials were missing. I pulled out one and read the label.

My stomach flipped a somersault.

"What is this?" I held out the vial, hoping I wasn't seeing what I thought I was seeing.

Luna squinted at the small glass container. "Oh, that's Bitsie's Botox. She's addicted to that stuff."

All those curiously blank facial expressions suddenly made sense.

"I've told her she doesn't need it," Luna added, still sifting through papers, "but she's convinced it makes her look younger. She stocks up in Mexico whenever she's down there. It's cheaper if you buy it on that side of the border. Anyway, it's probably best if you don't let on that you found her fountain of youth."

Unfortunately, if my suspicions were right, what I was holding was a lot more than that. I slipped the vial back into the box. "We have to find Bitsie."

"I know." Luna was now searching through the desk drawers. "This really isn't like her. Usually, she leaves me a note right here if she's going out." She tapped the side of the computer screen, and the motion made the crooning Elvis screensaver disappear.

Luna stared at the map that was there now.

"What is that?" I asked.

"I'm not sure. It looks like she was getting directions."

I peered over her shoulder and my pulse quickened. I recognized that address. It was Gunther Vernon's, and suddenly, it all made sense.

"I forgot my car is parked at Malone's. I'm going to run back and get it."

Luna swiveled around. "Now? What about Aneksi?"

"If she's with Bitsie, I'm sure she's all right."

Luna frowned, trying to process my quick change of heart. "Yeah, I'm sure she is. Are you all right?"

No. Not in the least.

What I said was, "Of course I am. Why wouldn't I be?" Before she could list the reasons, I hurried to the door, adding, "I'll just a few minutes. Lickety-split."

Lickety-what? I knew I sounded like a loon, but I didn't care. I had to get to that house.

I DON'T KNOW what I expected to find when I rolled up to that monstrosity of a home, but an empty driveway and dark windows wasn't it.

Had I been wrong to think Bitsie was bringing Aneksi here? Was this just another wild goose chase?

The vials I'd discovered in her office suggested a new possibility in the murders of Gunther and Martin, but the more I considered it, the more doubts I had. Bitsie hardly seemed to know Gunther.

Luna, on the other hand, knew all about Gunther's shady business dealings. Was that a motive? Maybe. But then, why kill Martin? It still didn't add up.

And what about Professor Omar? He was involved somehow, and he still had Stirling.

All these secrets and motives swirled around my brain and made my head hurt. I still didn't trust my own instincts, but I also couldn't take my concerns to the detective. Especially not after the mess I'd made at the diner.

Maybe Luna was right. Maybe I needed a nap. Or a hot bath. Or both.

Both sounded really nice.

Once I found Aneksi, that was what I would do. Relax and forget this whole mess, then maybe the world would make sense.

But I had to find Aneksi first, and this seemed like the best place to start.

After I let myself through the creaky iron gate, I searched the perimeter for signs of Bitsie and Aneksi. There weren't any. The house appeared as desolate as it had on that first, dreadful visit. At least it was daylight, but a cold shudder still crept down my spine.

I tried to ignore it as I worked my way toward the backyard, on the lookout for any signs of life. Something caught my eye midway down the side of the house. Someone had pulled the curtains closed over the window in Gunther's study. It had been open before. I was sure of it.

Was someone inside? Could it be Bitsie?

The window was too high to see in, so I circled around to the backyard. That was when I discovered a broken pane in one of the French doors. It was the pane closest to the lock, and it looked like it had been done so someone could reach in and open the door.

My first instinct was to call the police, but the more powerful instinct was to save Aneksi. I knew she was in there. I could feel it like a thousand tiny ants marching along my arms and legs. She needed my help.

Carefully, and as silently as I could manage, I pushed the door open and slipped inside. Inside, nothing moved. Nothing made a peep. The only sound was the pounding of my own heart. Slowly, I ventured toward Gunther's office.

The door was closed, but light seeped into the dim hallway from beneath it. I pressed my ear to the wood and made out a low murmuring that sounded like a chant or a prayer, followed by a long, harsh scraping of metal against metal.

Then a faint but familiar meow.

Aneksi!

I fought the urge to barge in and fetch her. Recklessness could get her hurt, or worse. So, slowly, ever so slowly, I turned the brass knob and inched open the door.

Inside, dozens of flickering candles had been arranged around the room. Some thick, some thin, some tall, some short. Amid the chaotic shadows of the dancing flames, I could see the room's desk had been pushed back, the mess on the floor had been cleared away, and the rug had been rolled up and pushed against the wall to reveal the wood planks beneath.

At the very center of the room, more flickering candles formed a circle and within it stood a golden birdcage. Sitting serenely in that cage, staring back at me with two piercing blue eyes, was that familiar and adorable bundle of gray fluff.

I pushed the door another inch and looked around for Bitsie, but Aneksi appeared to be entirely alone. It gave me courage.

"It's all right, furball," I cooed as I padded across the floor to collect her. "I'll get you out of that—"

The sight of a pair of sensible women's shoes poking out from behind the desk stopped me short.

As much as I wanted to grab Aneksi and run out of there, I had to help this woman. I moved closer and saw a pair of loose, gray pants, then a white blouse. The woman's arms were outstretched, as though she had fallen, but she was motionless, her expression blank, her eyes closed.

It was Eva Henriksen. But was she alive? Was she dead?

I inched closer to check for a pulse, but a quick thud stopped me.

Before I could turn to see what it was, something slammed the back of my head with terrible force. I stumbled forward, until the ground shot up to meet my chin and everything faded into inky black oblivion.

CHAPTER TWENTY-EIGHT

No Ordinary Cat

SEARING PAIN PULLED me back to consciousness. It seemed to be coming from the back of my head, but when I tried to lift my hand to rub the spot, I couldn't move. Somehow, I was sitting in a wooden chair in Gunther's study with each wrist tied to the chair's arms. When I tried to move my feet, I discovered they were tie-wrapped, too.

Everything was blurry, but I could make out the birdcage in front of me, and Aneksi's tiny, fuzzy form within it. She sat upright, watching me intently.

"What happened?" My voice scratched over my dry tongue.

I thought that kitten might tell me, but the voice that answered wasn't hers. It came from behind me.

"Finally," Bitsie snapped. She walked into the circle of candles and glared down at me. "Tell me how it works. How does she do it?"

What was she talking about? "How does who do what?"

She skewered me with a wild gaze. This wasn't the calm

and pleasant Bitsie I knew. Her forehead and cheeks were still unnaturally smooth, but hatred radiated off her like heat from a flame. "Don't play dumb. I know all about this little cat of yours. Cleopatra's cat, that's what Martin called her. The cat who's going to make me immortal." She glared back at Aneksi. "Aren't you, kitty cat?"

I'd had the same suspicions about Aneksi, but hearing the claim aloud, it sounded ridiculous. "She's an alley cat. Just a regular cat."

Bitsie scoffed. "If you don't tell me what I want to know, I'll have no use for you. See poor Eva over there?" She jutted her chin toward the body behind the desk. "I had no more use for her and look where it got her. Stupid woman. She thought she could scare me by threatening to go to the police. I could have easily pinned the whole thing on her, but it wasn't worth the trouble. You know, she was quite willing to lie to the police about you." She chuckled, a low, guttural, sound that set every one of my nerves on edge.

"Why? I don't even know her." I wanted to keep this crazy woman talking. Adelaide Morris always kept her captors talking. As long as they were doing that, they weren't killing, and right now, that was all I cared about.

Bitsie backed away. "Don't you see? That was the beauty of my plan. It had nothing to do with you. She hated Gunther, and I don't blame her. He made her life miserable. He made her run his errands, clean up after him, wait on him hand and foot. She even had to pick up his cheeseburgers from Malone's. That one happened to work in my favor. Those cheeseburger runs so often coincided with my lunchtime visits. She and I got to talking one day, you know, being two ladies of a certain age, and one thing led to another. When Martin told me what he was up to, he didn't know I already knew all about his new business partner."

"He told you what he'd done?"

Her eyes opened wide, and her hands flew to her chest dramatically. "Oh, Martin! What did you do? No, say it isn't so!" She smirked at her play acting. "He told me enough. The vent helped with the rest. Martin and Stirling both conducted very informative telephone calls in that office, but Martin especially. He was up to all sorts of mischief when Stirling wasn't around. So, yes, I knew exactly what he was doing. Oh, what's wrong, Rebecca? Did I fool you?"

She only pretended to wait for an answer before cackling with amusement. "Don't feel too badly about it. I'm an actor, after all. We lie for a living. You know, once that bag of fur works her magic, I think I might head back to Hollywood. With a new name and a new face, I'll be unstoppable."

"So that's why you had to get rid of Martin, too?"

"Of course. Once you helped me find him, that is. I really must thank you for that. I couldn't risk him ruining my plans. He might have figured out I was actually Gunther's mystery buyer. Or maybe not. You never questioned that call from Gunther, did you?" She straightened. Her jaw tensed.

"I have Cleopatra's cat. I must speak to your grandfather."

There was that strange accent again. No wonder I didn't recognize it. It was as fake as Bitsie's friendship.

She relaxed and laughed. "So gullible. So easy."

"You were good." I hated giving her a compliment, but I had to keep her talking. "What I don't get is why you didn't take the cat when you had the chance."

"You don't think I tried?" Rage flared in her eyes, but there was only the slightest wrinkle at the farthest edges of her forehead. "That idiot Gunther struck me when he felt the injection in his neck. He threw Cleopatra's cat at me, and it broke the stupid thing."

"That's why you called the shop and pretended to be Gunther." Until that moment, it hadn't made sense. But she had been desperate. Her chance at immortality was slipping through her fingers, and she hoped Stirling could fix it. "Now you have Aneksi, but you don't know how to make her powers work. You planted the address, so I would find it. You wanted me to follow you here."

Bitsie walked around to Eva and stared down at the life-less body. "Cleaning up loose ends. When the police find you both here, the cat and I will be long gone, and it will look like you killed Eva and then yourself. I'll make sure of that. But first, there's the matter of making that thing do her job." She stared at Aneksi, who sat primly, watching us. "I want you to tell me how it works. How do I harness that cat's power? Martin mentioned that blue glass skull and the old book of symbols. I gave them both to the cat, but she's ignoring them. What else do I need to do?"

"I have no idea." That was the truth. Despite my belief that Aneksi was no ordinary cat, I didn't know if she was immortal or if she could bestow that gift on anyone else. "Have you tried asking her?"

It wasn't sarcasm, but Bitsie's sneer told me she'd taken it that way. She raised her hand to strike me, but before her palm connected with my cheek, a sudden creak and crash stopped her.

Behind Bitsie, Aneksi's golden cage was gone. In its place was a pile of twisted and tangled metal spokes. Where was Aneksi?

In my peripheral vision, I caught a dark shadow racing through the room. When it stopped behind the woman, I couldn't believe what I was seeing, because what it looked like was a gray and black striped tiger as large as the desk with luminescent blue eyes that were staring directly at Bitsie.

My captor staggered back from the animal but didn't take her eyes off it. "Where did this monster come from?" Fear made her voice shrill. "Is this your doing?"

Did she think I could summon something like that? When I tried to push the chair back, away from the creature, it looked at me squarely with those giant eyes and held my gaze. I knew I should be afraid, but I wasn't. Not in the least.

"I've never seen that animal in my life," I said calmly.

The massive cat's gaze remained on me and … did it wink? That was when I noticed a familiar black stripe running down the back of its head. "Aneksi?"

Bitsie spun around. "Call it off. I'm warning you…"

Was laughter coming from that monstrous feline? When it subsided, the animal locked gazes with Bitsie. "This human holds no power over me."

That was Aneksi's voice. Deeper and more commanding, but definitely hers.

Bitsie stared into those hypnotic eyes and stammered before uttering, "You can talk?"

Tiger Aneksi sat back and licked her paw, the same way kitten Aneksi did. "Madame, do you doubt your own ears? Mistress Cleopatra was right. Humans can be so pitiful."

Bitsie clutched her chest as though she were struggling to breathe. She turned to me. "Is this some kind of a prank?"

Tiger Aneksi stretched and stalked closer to Bitsie. When she'd backed the woman against a cabinet, the animal lifted her nose to sniff Bitsie's cheeks before pulling back slightly. "I assure you, stupid woman, I am neither a joke nor a prank. But if you truly want my gift, you must look into my eyes."

Bitsie's glance slid from the animal's mouth, where fangs protruded on each side, up to her blue eyes. Bitsie's eyes widened as their gazes met.

"Yes, look deeply," the feline said. "Do you see what you desire?"

A shadow passed over Bitsie's expression. It went from its strained state to something more oblivious. Her shoulders and neck went slack, and she stood utterly still.

The big cat turned to me. "She will bother you no more."

"Is it really you, Aneksi?"

The animal's lips curled into a smile. "Must you ask?"

I knew it was her, but I didn't understand how it was possible. How was this creature the same sweet kitten curled beside my bed?

"Let me help with those." The cat moved closer, bared her fearsome fangs, and lowered them to my wrists, sliding one into the space between the plastic zip tie and my skin. The sharp tooth sawed effortlessly through one binding and then the other, before moving to my ankles to free me.

"Thank you, furball." I slid my hand between her fuzzy ears and scratched the silky spot on top of her head. She nuzzled against me and purred a diesel-engine purr. I gestured at Bitsie. "Does she need a doctor?"

The cat swung her head back to the older woman and wrapped her tail around her paws. "She will be fine. We should leave before she awakes, however."

I looked around the room and spied my purse in a corner. "I think I better stay here. People will have questions."

A few minutes after I called 911, sirens wailed down the street. Detective Devon didn't come alone, but he was the first one through the door. If it wasn't already unlocked, I was pretty sure he would have broken it down.

He entered with his pistol raised, but when he saw me near the study, he lowered it. "Are you all right? Are you hurt?"

I didn't want to take my eyes off Bitsie, who was still standing in that trance-like state, or Eva Henriksen, who was still lying on the floor. Neither had moved, but they were both breathing. I'd checked.

"I'm fine. They've been like this since I called you. I don't know what happened."

It was the truth, sort of, and there was no one around to dispute it. Aneksi had slipped out the back door. I didn't know where she went or how she could go anywhere looking the way she did, but I trusted she knew what she was doing.

"Bitsie was going to kill me." Somehow, saying it aloud made it all the more real. Like living through a nightmare.

Detective Devon pulled the handcuffs from his pocket, and for the first time, I was glad to see them. He snapped them around Bitsie's wrists. She hardly moved as he did it. Instead, she stared at him like she didn't know who he was or what he was doing. Then her head tilted to the side and in a dreamy voice, she asked, "Did you see it? It was beautiful. So beautiful…"

Whatever she'd seen in Aneksi's eyes had really done a number on her.

The detective had a firm grip on Bitsie, but he was eying me. "Why were you here, exactly? I saw your car outside.

Did you come on your own? Did she lure you here?"

"I thought she had my cat."

He looked around. "Did she? I don't see a cat."

How could I tell him she'd slipped out after shifting into a tiger and saving me from this lunatic? I couldn't, but I had to tell him something.

"Rebecca, my dear, are you all right?"

Stirling pushed past two uniformed officers standing at the door and barreled toward the detective and me. He was holding something in both arms, and when I saw what it was, I nearly cried with relief.

"Aneksi!" I rushed to meet him in the hallway and took the cat from him. I held her so closely, I could feel the beat of her tiny heart. "Aneksi, where have you been?"

"Mr. Cuthbert, it's good to see you," Detective Devon said over Bitsie's head. "Rebecca was worried about you. She thought you might be under some—"

He stopped when the professor's large figure appeared in the doorway and made his way inside. "There you are, Stirling. You still have the cat, don't you? Ah, I see you do. Hello, Rebecca. Good to see you. All is well, I trust?"

I stammered something close to a greeting. I didn't know why they were here or where they had been, but I was thankful that both Stirling and Aneksi were unharmed.

"Did you find what you were looking for?" the detective asked.

I was about to answer when I realized his question wasn't

directed at me.

"Yes. Well, as it turns out, it was all a misunderstanding," my grandfather rushed to say.

"It was?" The professor asked skeptically.

"It was." My grandfather shot a warning glance at the much larger man.

"Of course it was," the professor grumbled.

"Good to hear," the detective said.

"Yes. Absolutely," Stirling said, but he wasn't paying attention to the detective anymore. He was watching Bitsie glance around the room like she didn't know where she was.

Her befuddled gaze landed on the detective. "What's happening here?"

Before he could answer, Stirling marched up to her. "Did you intend to harm my granddaughter? And what about that poor woman?" He gestured to the desk, where the paramedics had strapped an oxygen mask over Eva's face. "What in the world did you hope to accomplish?"

She slanted a venomous stare at him. "You wouldn't understand. Men never do." She jutted her chin at me. "She won't even understand for at least another twenty years. Unless that cat of hers saves her from that final indignity."

"Keep Aneksi out of this," I shot back. "You're lucky she didn't…" I stopped when I saw Stirling's eyes straining with an unspoken warning.

"Didn't what?" Detective Devon asked, suddenly curious.

Stirling came up beside me and touched my elbow. "Detective, my granddaughter has suffered a terrible ordeal. I think you and I can both agree she needs to rest."

"Of course," the detective said. "This has been ... a lot."

"Then, with your permission, I'd like to take her home."

Boy, he was really working the sympathy card. I tried to do my part by looking as pitiful as possible. I snuggled Aneksi.

For a minute, I thought Detective Devon was going to shut my grandfather down. But instead, he gave me a sad, almost sweet smile. "Yes, that would be fine. But I do have additional questions. Can we meet tomorrow?"

I swallowed the snide response that sprang to mind. "I can be at your office by eight. Will that work?"

Aneksi squirmed in my arms and meowed her displeasure. I ignored her and kept the smile plastered on my face.

"Seven-thirty would be better," he said.

"Perfect." I pushed by Bitsie and pulled Stirling along with me before I or Aneksi said something I'd regret.

CHAPTER TWENTY-NINE

On the Record

DETECTIVE DEVON APPEARED behind the low swinging door that separated the police station's lobby from the official area behind the counter and waved me through.

"You came. Guess I can cancel that all-points bulletin."

I ignored his sarcasm. "I set an extra alarm especially for you." I'd actually set five on my phone, programed to go off at five-minute intervals so I wouldn't sleep through our meeting. One perp walk out of my grandfather's shop was enough for me, thank you.

"You planning to drink both of those cups of coffee?" He glanced at the paper cups I was holding.

"There's only one coffee, and it's for you." I extended the cup.

After he took it, he peeked under the lid.

"Four creamers, no sugar," I said, answering his unspoken question.

He smiled. "You remembered."

"It's hard to forget."

"True." He chuckled. "What's in your cup?"

"Tea."

His brows pulled together. "Could have sworn you were a coffee drinker."

"Me too. Stirling must be rubbing off on me." Since tea was all Stirling stocked, I was drinking a lot of it. This morning, when I stopped at a coffee place on my way in, I'd been drawn to the selection of teas. The vanilla black tea had sounded interesting. So far, I had no regrets.

When we reached the detective's desk, I mustered the courage to ask the question I'd been dying to ask. "What did Bitsie tell you?"

All night, I'd lain in bed staring at the ceiling and going over what she'd told me. I knew she was the killer, but would the detective take my word for it? He'd doubted me before.

"Ms. Baynor didn't have much to say," he said, "but Ms. Henriksen has been quite talkative."

"She has?" The woman was barely conscious when I'd left.

"She was nearly a victim herself, so that was probably pretty motivating."

"But she was also a coconspirator. You know that, right? That's why she lied about me. Did she tell you she lied? I was not at that house before Gunther's murder."

His hands went up to stop me. "She did. She claims she didn't know Ms. Baynor planned to kill anyone, only that Ms. Baynor intended to steal an Egyptian statue that ended up breaking during an altercation. Ms. Henriksen said it had belonged to your grandfather and that Ms. Baynor was trying to retrieve it for him. When Gunther tried to stop her from taking it, Bitsie said she fought back in self-defense."

"You don't believe that, do you? That's not what she was doing."

"That's for a jury to decide, but it's not going to look good that she happened to have a lethal dose of Botox in a syringe all ready to go. That reeks of premeditation."

"And Martin?"

"Right, two victims. Same MO. She's going to go away for a very long time."

The dark cloud hovering over me brightened a little. But something still didn't make sense. The afternoon we'd had ice cream, I'd been on the phone with him. Not her. "How did she find out where Martin was hiding? I never shared his location with her."

He sipped his coffee. "That one stumped us, too, until we searched her shop. We found the pad of paper where she'd used the old pencil-shading trick to reveal an address."

"Pencil-shading trick?"

He pulled his notepad from his breast pocket and flipped to a blank page. He grabbed a pencil from the desk and wrote a phone number. Then he ripped off that page and ran the side of the pencil lead over the corresponding spot. Like magic, the numbers appeared. He tapped it with the pencil. "The page with the information was gone, but she still got what she needed."

I stared at it. "You know, all that time, I thought she was trying to get close to me to get to Stirling. I thought she was interested in him. I was so stupid."

"You aren't stupid. You can't think that way. Trusting people and seeing the best in them isn't a flaw. It's a gift."

I didn't know what to say. It was the nicest thing anyone had said to me in a long time. All I could manage was, "Thank you."

"You know," he said. "There is something I wanted to ask you."

I braced. Did he know I wasn't telling the whole truth?

"I've been thinking about the zip ties she used on you. I'm curious how you broke them. They're pretty tough. Did you have a knife?"

I didn't want to lie, but I also couldn't tell him I had help from a seven-hundred-pound tiger. I tried to think of something intelligent yet evasive to say, but what tumbled out of my mouth was, "I didn't use a knife."

If only that could be the end of it, but I wasn't so lucky. I was never that lucky.

"We found the severed zip-ties, and the cuts were so clean. What did you use?"

He wanted an answer, and I didn't have one. Not one he'd believe.

Was it getting hotter in here? Sweat beaded on the back of my neck, beneath my hair. He stared at me, waiting, and I had … nothing.

Instead of getting angry, his expression softened. "I know this can be hard. Just tell me what you remember."

"But I don't remember. It's all just a blur." Aneksi-tiger had been a blur when she ran around the room, so it wasn't a total lie, right?

His mouth quirked with disappointment. "Is there anything you remember? We'd like to get your account on record, if possible."

A terrifying idea struck me. "You're not going to let her go, are you? If I can't remember?"

"No, she's not going anywhere. It would be nice to know how her scheme fell apart, but it isn't essential."

That was a relief.

"I mean," he added sheepishly, "the important thing is you're all right. That's what really matters."

It was a nice thing to say and surprisingly out of character. I was about to say so when he turned away. A red flush crept over his neck and his ears.

Was he blushing?

"Are you all right?" I tried to suck back my grin.

He straightened, and that ubiquitous scowl returned. "Yeah, I mean, of course. Thank you for coming in this morning." He glanced down at his cup. "And thank you for the coffee."

That was it, I guess. I was being dismissed.

I stood. "You're welcome. I guess I'll be heading back to

the shop." Why was my mouth suddenly drier than Death Valley? I sipped my tea, but it didn't help. "Thanks for your time, detective." I hitched my purse up to my shoulder and turned toward the corridor.

All night and all morning, I'd been dreading this interview, and now I didn't want to leave. What was wrong with me? It took all my willpower to keep walking.

"Rebecca?"

The word stopped me cold. I turned back.

"Would you mind if I came by the shop in a few days? To make sure you're … you know, that everything's all right."

This time I didn't hide my grin. "I wouldn't mind at all."

CHAPTER THIRTY

A New Mystery

A S I ENTERED Cuthbert Exotic Antiques, the door chime woke Aneksi from where she was napping between a pair of King Tut bookends and an African fertility figure displayed in the shop window.

"Back already?" She lazily stretched one front leg then the other.

My panic must not have escaped her notice because she shook her small, fuzzy head with amused exasperation. "Do not worry. No one is here. I know the rules."

The rules, which Stirling insisted upon, were that she was allowed to roam the shop freely during the day as long as she didn't knock anything over, did her business in the litter box in the washroom, and remained completely silent when anyone else was present.

In the evenings, she returned with me to his apartment and remained in the guest bedroom. After a week of this, we'd settled into a comfortable routine.

Even Stirling was coming around. A few times, I'd

caught him with Aneksi on his lap while he worked on the computer. I'd even overheard him a couple of times trying to coax information from her about particular Egyptian antiques and artifacts.

"Is that you, Rebecca?" Stirling called from the office.

When I called back that it was, he stepped into the hallway with a finger hooked behind his bow tie, trying to loosen it.

"What's up?" I tried to sound casual, but those rigid shoulders and his creased brow worried me. Something was on his mind, and I had a feeling I knew what it was.

I'd been his guest for nearly three weeks, and while he never pressed me about how long I intended to stay, I knew I was in danger of wearing out my welcome if I hadn't already.

The trouble was, I didn't want to leave. All I had to go back to was that big, empty house and that big, empty bookstore. They were home when my parents were alive, but that all changed after the accident. Now they were simply cold reminders of what I'd lost.

And it wasn't just the loss of my parents. I'd also lost Mason and Lacey. I'd lost the future I'd been planning for my whole life. In Elk Pass, if I wasn't Bill and Sharon Cuthbert's daughter, or Mason Morretti's girl, or Lacey Gatz's best friend, I didn't know who I was. Maybe I was nobody.

Here in Citrus Grove, it was different. I could be anybody. I could just be me.

Despite all the craziness, despite nearly being arrested, I liked it here. I liked Stirling's quirky little shop. I liked this quirky little town. I liked this strange cat and my strange grandfather, who I shuddered to think I'd ever considered a murder suspect. I even liked Professor Omar, now that I knew he hadn't kidnapped my grandfather but had been helping him search Gunther's neighborhood for whatever might have escaped from that broken vessel—which was as much as Stirling had admitted even after he learned the truth himself.

But I knew the day would come when Stirling would hire a new manager and my visit would have to end.

That wincing expression on his face told me that day was probably today.

"I want to discuss something with you, if you have a moment," he said.

My grandfather was always a bit formal, but when he was nervous or uncomfortable, it was worse.

"Sure, I'm not going anywhere." I cringed at my poor choice of words.

"I was thinking it's about time to get three-C back on the market, now that it's been cleared out."

Three-C had been Bitsie Baynor's apartment. After she was arrested, she had asked Stirling to send her things to a storage unit Luna had arranged for her. I'd overheard the phone call, which was how I discovered Stirling owned the Heritage View Apartments. The man truly was full of surprises.

"I'm sure you won't have any trouble finding a new tenant." Maybe I'd gotten lucky. Maybe he was still too busy to think about getting his guest bedroom back.

"You're probably right, but it occurred to me you might like it. I mean, if you were intending to stay awhile."

Like I said, the man was full of surprises.

"Are you asking if I want the apartment?"

"Before you say anything, you should know it's only a studio. There is a nice-sized bathroom, however."

The more he said, the more it sounded like he was trying to talk me into it.

I waved my hands to make him stop. "I can't afford an apartment. I don't have a job."

He pushed his glasses up the ridge of his nose. "I believe we could work something out. I still need a manager. The job can be yours if you are amenable to the idea."

"Really? I mean, are you serious?"

It sounded too good to be true, and in my experience, that usually meant it was. Things like this—really amazing things—never happened to me. There had to be a catch.

"I am serious," he said. "I haven't had family around for many years, and I've truly enjoyed getting to know you. I see a bit of my son in you, and perhaps a little of myself as well. There is no doubt you are a Cuthbert. I won't force the legacy upon you. I won't risk alienating you as I did with my son. But your help with Cleopatra's cat has been invaluable. I would welcome any level of involvement you desire."

Aneksi must have heard us talking about her because I felt a warm, furry body brush against my ankles. It was her silent but not subtle way of letting me know she wanted attention. Like the good human she was training me to be, I bent down, scooped her up, and scratched her between the ears.

"What do you mean? Aneksi seems happy enough here."

"Happy enough, yes," she said as my fingertips brushed her head. "A little lower. Oh yes, there."

"She does seem to have adjusted," Stirling said. "It's a relief, too, because our little genie can't exactly go back into her bottle. But there is more to be done."

"More? I thought it was settled?" I stopped scratching, and Aneksi nudged my hand to keep it moving.

"Aneksi is settled, yes, but she wasn't the only artifact Martin took."

I didn't like the sound of that. "What are you saying?"

He hooked that finger under his collar again. "There are other items of a more, shall we say, problematic nature that must be located."

"Problematic as in…" I couldn't bring myself to say the word.

"Cursed. Yes. It's an unfortunate term, but I'm afraid it applies. You have already done so much, for which I am and always will be grateful. I understand completely if this is asking too much, but you have shown such—"

As his words continued to tumble out, my mind reeled. I knew I should be alarmed. I should be running for the hills, or at least back to the Rocky Mountains. I should want nothing at all to do with what he was not-so-subtly proposing.

But that wasn't my reaction at all. The feeling in my stomach wasn't fear. It was curiosity, excitement, and something else. Adelaide Morris would call it the lure of a new mystery.

Whatever it was, I knew in that moment I wasn't going anywhere. This was exactly where I wanted to be. With Stirling, with Aneksi, and with a purpose I could feel all the way down to my toes.

"Are you all right, Rebecca?" Stirling stepped closer. "You look a bit flushed."

"I feel fine," I said after a deep breath. "Actually, I've never felt better."

The End

EXCLUSIVE PERK: FREE PURR-FECT RELIC NOVELLA

Grab *Dead End Date*, a free novella available exclusively to members of my Cozy Readers Club, to find out how Rebecca and Aneksi hunt down another killer during Rebecca's first date with Detective Nick Devon at Citrus Grove's hottest new nightspot!

When you join me and other cozy mystery readers in the Cozy Readers Club, you'll also have access to free puzzles, book-related recipes, behind-the-scenes tidbits, and loads of other bonus content. Sign up at DeAnnaDrake.com/join.

It's free and easy, and you won't miss any of the fun!

One last thing...

Thank you for taking the time to read *Paws, Claws & Curses*, the first book in the Purr-fect Relic Cozy Mystery series! If Rebecca and Aneksi have earned a soft spot in your book-loving heart, it would mean so much to me if you could jot a few words in a review at Amazon or Goodreads, or both! Good reviews and positive word of mouth are extremely helpful to an author and always deeply appreciated.

If you enjoyed *Paw, Claws, and Curses*,
you'll love the next book in….

A Purr-fect Relic Cozy Mystery series

Book 1: *Paw, Claws, and Curses*

Book 2: *Hisses, Hexes, and Homicide*

Book 3: *Furballs and Felonies*

Available now at your favorite online retailer!

About the Author

DeAnna Drake is an award-winning author who writes witty and whimsical cozy mysteries filled with magical animals and feisty heroines who are always striving to balance the scales of justice in an offbeat world.

Under different names, DeAnna writes young-adult fantasy fiction, contemporary romances, and historical novels set in the Victorian and Edwardian eras.

When she isn't plotting new adventures for her characters, she's a craft addict, drinks too much tea, binge watches crime dramas, and escapes to Disneyland whenever she can.

She lives in Southern California with her family, which includes her two favorite people and one ridiculously pampered border collie. Learn more at DeAnnaDrake.com.

Thank you for reading

Paw, Claws, and Curses

If you enjoyed this book, you can find more from all our great authors at TulePublishing.com, or from your favorite online retailer.

TULE
PUBLISHING

www.ingramcontent.com/pod-product-compliance
Lightning Source LLC
Chambersburg PA
CBHW020100180626
46812CB00006B/2412